LOST IN TRANSITION

Fighting Words is a creative writing centre, established by Roddy Doyle and Sean Love. It opened in January 2009 and aims to help students of all ages to develop their writing skills and to explore their love of writing. It provides story-writing fieldtrips for primary school groups, creative writing workshops for secondary students, and seminars, workshops and tutoring for adults. All tutoring is free.

www.fightingwords.ie

Scoil Chaitríona is a co-educational second level Gaelscoil in Glasnevin, Dublin 9.

LOST IN TRANSITION

FOURTH YEAR STUDENTS,
SCOIL CHAITRÍONA,
GLASNEVIN

INTRODUCTION BY ANNE ENRIGHT

FIGHTING WORDS
THE WRITE TO RIGHT

A Fighting Words Book

Lost in Transition is published in May 2011 by Fighting Words

© Individual authors 2011

Editors: Ciara Doorley and Daniel Bolger

Set in Palatino and Book Antiqua

Cover Design: www.pcc.ie

Printed by: Naas Printing Ltd, Kildare

Fighting Words,
Behan Square,
Russell Street,
Dublin 1

www.fightingwords.ie

ISBN: 978-0-9568326-0-3

CONTENTS

INTRODUCTION

I still have the pieces I wrote when I was fifteen and sixteen – not the geography notes, but the love poems and ardent prose fragments and maybe even a story or two. It is all up in the attic somewhere, lurking in a green vinyl binder, with Led Zeppelin lyrics and quotes from Shelley doodled on the cover. I am too embarrassed to read any of it now, but I would never throw it away. I am saving it for my dotage, perhaps, when, by losing my mind, I come back to myself again.

I knew I would hang on to it. I thought, at the time, that this was the most important stuff I could ever write. This is what makes it embarrassing, but also – yes – important. There was something essential about the words I put down on paper in those years. It was at that moment when the raw need to write, to say the thing that needed to be said, was overwhelming. And I didn't have a clue what to do with it. I was compelled to say something, but I could not say what that something was; I didn't know how it might be shaped, or what form it could take. The miracle, with early work, is the way brute necessity wins. Talent pulls itself up by its own bootstraps. You make a story even though you do not know how to make a story. Or sometimes . . . a teacher, a chance remark, a series of workshops in, for example, Fighting Words, helps you break into that circle – gives you air, tools, hints, a leg up, a way to proceed.

The amount of pure learning that goes into a writer's first and early fictions is amazing. Reading the work in this collection is watching something grow in front of your eyes – the push of feeling, and the creak of the writer's mind getting bigger; it is here on every page.

Stories, by definition, are about things that matter – they matter enough for us to write them down. Adolescence, as I remember it, was a time when things really mattered to me: perhaps because of this, the books I read in those years stayed with me for the rest of my life. Fighting Words flourishes on that intensity, and honours it, because no writer ever outgrows this first stage – they only pretend to.

The stories in this collection share a sense of urgency that gives me hope for the future. They are about the stuff of ordinary life: fighting with your mother, falling for a guy with floppy hair, being bullied, being talked about. They are often very dramatic, with adopted children and lost children, coincidences, madness, disasters, death. They are also about the stuff of dreams: there are hints of the thriller or of science fiction and a couple of high-concept tales that owe as much to Borges as to Hollywood.

There is nothing easy about the choice of style. In each tale, you see the story struggle to attain its proper form. You can see the writers looking for events that are big enough to match their feelings, and then keep them credible through plot and style.

But no matter how near or how far they are from what might be called 'ordinary life' what these stories share is an thrilling sense of voice. 'Blood everywhere,' says the Irish soldier in 'The Fighting Irish' by Cameron Ó Fiannaí, 'and men who I'd spent years in the army with were lying face down in the dirt.' This story is set in the Congo, but there is equal accuracy in the voice of the teenager in Rebecca Miley's 'There's No Romance in Ballymun'. 'Lauren went on a mad one,' she says, and,'Of course, Jordan denied it down to the ground.'

If these students have learned anything, it is how to start a story with a bang – sometimes literally. Dearbhla de Búrca Ní Bhaoill's *'Famille de Bizarre'* opens with the words, 'Water shot at me, its force winding me so hard I fell off the chair.' This lively, semi-satirical view of a French exchange, starts with a broken tap and water shooting 'up my blue pyjama sleeve'. 'It hit me,' is the first thing we hear from Seona Ní Nualláin's narrator in 'Room 21', a story of a lost mother, which ends with the lovely cadence of: 'She turned back, stared, and saw nothing.' Mothers loom large in these stories – and the way you might fight with them. Caoimhe Ní Mhúineacháin's ironically titled 'Domestic Bliss' surges with the unfairness of family life, while Saoirse Ní hAgáin's heroine in 'Shades of Grey', feels out of place in a family she does not recognise as her own. There is accidental incest (or near incest) in Nadine Ní Mhaonaigh's 'Forbidden Love?' and the emptiness at the centre of the whole family project plays out as drama in Kevin Ó Laighin's 'Scattered'. This story ends with a moment that might be said to state the whole problem, as a woman puts her hand on her pregnant belly and feels 'the unforgettable sensation of a small purposeful kick.'

Éadaoin Ní Fhaoláin's 'Pretty Damn Wonderful' ends with the pretty damn wonderful line: 'My name is Evie, I'm nineteen years old, and I'm not going to die yet.' This story, with its big emotions and big events, is not afraid to seize life by the collar. The narrator has a major meltdown – and it helps. 'It was like those moments of screaming madness ripped up every thing that was holding me back.' Her fearlessness is typical, none of these young people avoid the big questions or the big themes. Kelsey Ní Dhúill's 'Moving On' is a careful study of love, loss and renewal. Clare Ní Mhuirí gives the subject of mourning a further twist as her character, Grace, descends into a witty kind of madness, losing herself in the character of Holly Golightly from *Breakfast at Tiffany's*. Oddness and insanity also figure in

Dónal Ó Rinn's 'Second Shadow', an uncanny tale with a slow reveal, which works close to the central character to great narrative effect. Madness was one of the great fears of my own adolescence, so these stories bring it all back. They also show the mixture of empathy and resistance that fiction does best – the way stories show us how not to grow up.

The amount of sympathy the writers show for the lives of their characters is great to see. Nathan Ó'Dúláinne's 'An Epic Dream' might be a bit mad, as we as we shift from one point of view to another and reality gives way – but it is also funny and clever and far from cold. 'Cop On' by Alex Ó Láighléis gives us another dreamscape, vividly realised and full of moral force and emotion.

Ciarán Ó Duibhghinn's 'Chronoshift' is a more controlled nightmare; a time travel thriller, which has, at its heart, the image of a man crying in a lift. These stories are interested in one of the most urgent narrative problems: time and what you can do with it on the page. Gareth Mac Coinn Mac Réamóinn 'Last Chance Saloon' starts on the echo of a shot, and it details the tiniest moment possible, which is the moment when a man dies.

All these stories work the sentences and pay close attention to language, but a couple are also interested in language for its own sake. 'Awakening' by Kevin Ó hÉanna deals with a false Utopia in which God, authority, and mankind have all become subsumed under the vague, all powerful word 'Man'. The concept in this writerly story works itself out, not just in the actions of the characters, but in the sentences themselves. Sadhbh Ní Bhroin Ní Riain's 'Fragmented' meanwhile, is the delicate tale of an ordinary telepath that is poetic in its lightness and intensity.

Alongside with these high concept stories are the low-concept, no-concept buccaneering naturalism of 'A Bloody Hammer in a Rusty Transit Van' by Stiofán Mac Giolla Rua and 'Everybody Loves Mondays' by Aarron Ó Hamiltúin:

tales with a bit of swagger that are interested in telling it like it is – or as it could be. There is the thriller 'One Day . . .' by Liam Ó Brádaigh, in which a policewoman secretly texts from a phone inside her pocket – a plot device as yet confined to the young (I look forward to seeing in next year's books).

It is the voices that really sing it out in these stories. The narrator of Sinéad Ní Normáin's 'Come Sit With Me' takes no prisoners. 'It was 1996,' says the opening paragraph. 'The year Veronica Guerin was shot dead in her car. The year when 2 became 1 for the Spice Girls and The Fugees were Killing us Softly.' The narrator is witty, fluent, interested in the real world – her main character is all this too, but he is also a bit slow on the uptake and the difference between them is where the story lies. Bríd Ní Chomáin, meanwhile, gives us four distinct voices in 'Missing': first is the restless, fretful voice of Mr Daly the school principle, then the unforgettably sweet, true tones of the missing girl's little sister. We approach the runaway through an account given by a homeless man, but all we get from the girl herself is the briefest note. 'And I was tired,' she writes. It is, finally, the sister we remember – with the sophisticated simplicity that distinguishes this story, she says: 'There's something about loving people – family, like, that makes you miss the bad things just as much as the good.' This problem – the problem of loving people – is on every page of this collection and it is tackled head on, with wit, inventiveness and great courage.

This is important work.

Everybody Loves Mondays

Aarron Ó Hamiltúin

It's a cold, dark, dreary Monday morning. The wind is blowing in a thick black sea fog. The rain is lashing down from the heavens.

An eerie silence is broken by a deep, harsh, depressed and drunken man's voice.

'D'ya have some change?' he asks.

'Yes,' replies Dave.

He makes no effort to reach into his pocket and says after a pause,

'Well?'

'What?' says the drunk, looking confused.

'Why are you still here?' says Dave.

'I asked you if you had some change.'

'Yeah, I do, I have loads.'

'Can I have some?'

'Who do you think you are? Asking me for money in these times, the recession like, are you for real? No one has money, actually why don't you give me money?' shouts Dave.

'Look man I'm sorry, but I don't wanna hear your life story I just want a euro like.'

'I'll kill you if you ask me that again right. I ought to kill yeh right now.'

'So, is that a yes?' says the drunk.

'Feck off away from me,' snarls Dave.

'Sorry.'

Dave opens the gate and walks into the yard. He is in fact the owner of Dave's Building and Roofing, Dublin's best builders and roofers – or so he says. You see, Dave started off with a ladder, a bike, and a hammer. Back then he was more of an anything-and-everything guy, he even sold stuff up at the Liberty Market of a Saturday. Eventually Dave's Building and Roofing was started.

He hurries in to the office. He's drenched.

'Bastardin' rain,' mutters Dave.

He lights the gas fire and sits down on an old wooden stool, it creaks from the strain. In the cold, damp, dreary office Dave tries turning on the computer. It doesn't work.

'Feck that Bill Gates chap anyway, all this technology's ruining the world. Back in my day there was no such thing as a Walkman.'

About an hour later, Dave's daughter Kim walks in.

'Where have you been, ye stupid eejit, you're late. What kinda secretary are ye?' shouts Dave.

'Feck off will yeh, first thing in the morning. What are yeh like, bleedin' animal!' screeches Kim.

'Shut it you and get to work.'

The phone rings, Kim answers.

'Hoi, Dave's Building and Roofing how can I . . . Oh, it's you.'

'Jesus Christ, who is it?' Dave demands.

'For *God's* sake, it's Paddy, he wants to know if he will come in today?'

'Don't use the *Lord's* name in vain, and no not today there's no bleedin' work happening.'

'Bye,' says Kim.

She hangs up the phone.

The rain is drumming against the window, quick,

constant taps getting louder and louder every minute, the door blows open with a bang and then it slams closed again.

'What's wrong with that computer, feckin' thing? It wouldn't work when I came in this morning.'

'Did yeh plug it in?' asks Kim

'Course I did, what d'ya take me for, a bleedin eejit?'

She walks over, picks up the plug and lets it dangle mid-air hanging just above her head. She plugs it in herself and says,

'Try it now.'

He presses the on button, sparks fly from the plug. Kim leaps away in fright, the plug ignites and she runs outside in a confused hurry.

A stack of pages instantly lights up. Dave jumps from his seat, he grabs the fire extinguisher from under his table, it's empty, he throws it away and grabs the pages, throws them outside in the rain and then kicks at the plug until the fire goes out, then he rips it out of the wall. Kim arrives back in gasping for breath.

'That nearly gave me a heart attack,' she says.

'What if that happened when I wasn't here? Would you have let the place burn down?'

'No, 'course not.'

'Why is it we have an empty fire extinguisher?'

'Don't start shoutin' at me, right, 'cause you were too cheap to buy a new one,' she snaps.

'I was busy,' says Dave, pretending to look offended. 'And why is it that the emergency sprinkler didn't work?'

'Cause the pipes broke in the January snow last year and you wouldn't pay to get dem fixed.'

'I was away.'

Shane comes in. He's seventeen, tall and skinny; left school to work when he was sixteen, drives a grey Micra and plays for the Ireland under-17s football team.

'What's that smell?' asks Shane.

'The computer went on fire.'

'*Cool.*'

'It's not *cool*,' roars Dave.

'What happened?' asks Shane

Dave completely ignores him.

'Go over to Jerry's shop and have a look at the roof. He rang on Saturday about a leak. Price the job and tell me first, he's a good friend of mine. Look after him will yeh?'

'Yep.'

It's nearly dark when Shane comes back.

'That weather's miserable, hasn't stopped raining all day,' moans Dave.

'Yeah, I saw thunder and lightning while I was drivin' back in the van.'

'Yeah, it's terrible. Anyway, how did ja get on at Jerry's shop?' asks Dave.

'It's just a hole in the roof, two new slates to be put on. With insurance and vat prices I'd say 350 euro.'

'Alright, I'll do it for 900 euro,' says Dave.

'What? It's only a tiny hole in the roof.'

'Sorry, you're right, 950 euro.'

'But I thought he was your friend?'

'Ahh now, I don't know him that well.'

'Alright, I'll give him the price,' Shane says reluctantly.

As Shane walks out Kim gets off the phone and says,

'Dave, the computer technician said not to use the computer, he'll be over tomorrow. It will cost 40 euro,' says Kim.

'Cancel it then, it's grand, I'll fix it myself.'

'You couldn't fix that computer if your life depended on it,' she laughs.

'Yes I could easily, watch I'll do it right now'

He smacks the computer a couple of times and then he plugs it in.

It works.

'See, it's grand. Now write an estimate for Jerry's shop for 1250 euro.'

'I thought it was for 950 euros?'

'Are you the boss or am I?'

'You are.'

'Then shut up, right.'

Next day, Dave gets up, makes himself a cup of tea and gets into his car; he's greeted by the orange fuel light the petrol meter's on empty he hits it a couple of times it doesn't move. He starts the car.

'Ahh, I'll just about make it.'

He drives through a puddle, soaking all the people at the bus stop and laughs. The traffic's terrible, with a stupid L driver blocking up everything. As he nears the yard Dave sees a plume of thick black smoke.

'Some stupid eejit must of started a fire, at least it's not me.'

He turns the corner and sees his yard ablaze. At first he's shocked, but then he thinks about the insurance money and his face lights up. Dave parks his car and waits; eventually a fireman approaches.

'You own that place there?'

'Yep.'

'We're doing all we can to put it out, but we're mainly just stopping it from spreading to the other houses.'

'Ok, d'ya know what started the fire?'

'Well, we think it was an electrical appliance of some sort.'

'Ok, thanks,' says Dave

He dials the number for the insurance company.

'Hello, Allianz Insurance, how can I help you?'

'I'd like to report an accident.'

'Ok, can I get your details first Mr . . . ?'

'Ryan, Dave Ryan.'

'One moment please, bear with me Mr Ryan.'

'Hurry up, I haven't got all day.'

'Sorry, Allianz Insurance would like to help you, but according to our records your balance is overdue by three years. Goodbye.'

'Noooo . . . wait a minute.'

Dave then dials Kim's number.

'You do not have sufficient credit to make this call.'

He hangs up and starts to look for change. Finding none, Dave sees a man who looks very familiar; he gets out of the car and says,

'Sorry have you got some change?'

'Yeh, I do, I've loads,' says the man. He continues walking.

 **Aarron Ó Hamiltúin is sixteen years old. He lives in Swords and plays football for Swords Manor FC. He enjoys playing guitar.**

Cop On

Alex Ó Láighléis

I looked around but nobody looked back. I was surrounded by the people I though I knew best, that I thought cared for me, but all I saw was pure disapproval. My name is Ruairi. I'm sixteen. I'm not very artistic or intellectual; I'm what you would call a waste of space. I see it as a lifestyle.

It all started when the Christmas tests results came back from school; a bunch of the lads and some girls from the school down the road decided to go to the woods just outside town. Everything was going to plan. We had the drink courtesy of Cam's older brother Leo; my mam and dad were going out with their friends 'til like 3 a.m., so no chance of being caught, and finally there were the birds, no night is the same if the girls aren't there. Everyone got off the bus in high spirits, most were happy with the scores they got in the tests. I, on the other hand, not very surprisingly, didn't do as well as everyone else. As we got to the river, people began to relax.

'Right lads, let's make tonight one to remember,' I said, as I opened my first can of Dutch Gold.

'Here, Ruairi, don't go overboard on the cans tonight right bud, remember what happened the last time.'

People started smirking and laughing at me. I know what they all think of me, but I'm fine with that.

'Don't worry about me,' I snarled back, 'you just worry about yourself.'

As the night wore on, more and more people began to drink way over the limit. By now the smell of the girls' overpowering perfume and the smell of vomit had taken hold of the camp. Down goes another, I thought to myself, as I threw a can onto the pile that was turning into a small landfill. I strolled over to the river to take a slash; I hadn't realised how badly I needed to go. I closed my eyes, relief coursed through my body, but sadly it was short-lived when I heard two shrieks coming from just in front of me.

'What the hell do you think you're doing, ya Muppet?' said a girl. 'Ya nearly went all over me!'

'Sorry about that,' I replied, trying to hide a smirk.

'Are you thick or what?'

'Look at him smiling, he doesn't even care the little rat,' said her friend. I turned around and walked over to John, who was hammered and talking to two very attractive girls. As soon as I opened my mouth John started slagging me off.

'So man, how did the tests go for you?' he said, knowing that I didn't do well at all.

'Em, not bad, I guess,' I replied.

'So, tell me, what did you get in maths?' he continued.

I didn't reply.

'No answer then?'

He and the girls started to laugh. The hell with this, I thought, and ran off into the woods by myself. I was still very drunk and had no clue where I was going, but then again I never really knew where I was going. I was happy being me, so what if I didn't have a plan for my life? I'll get by just fine.

The aromas of the forest engulfed me: the smell of the pine, the touch of the trees, and the cool night air rushing against my body. With all these sensations going through me, I don't know why, but the moss-covered forest floor looked too comfortable to pass up.

When I woke it was late evening and I was lying on the forest floor, smelling of the night before. It suddenly hit me that my mam must be worried that I never arrived home last night. I checked my pockets for my phone but it wasn't there anymore.

'Awww!' I screamed at the top of my lungs.

At least I still had my wallet.

I walked through the forest until I found the road. I stood at the bus stop for nearly an hour before the damn bus came. As the doors opened, I noticed that the bus man looked like he'd been out all night; he was clearly hungover.

'Em, does this bus not come every half hour?' I asked him.

'Look mate, I come when I come, OK?' he said.

He didn't seem to care if he was on time or not. I got on the bus and noticed there was only a drunk man sitting in what looked like his own urine. No people in suits going to work, or teenagers going into town with their friends; it was just me, the driver and the bum at the back of the bus. I paid my fare and sat down. Through the window I saw about three cars on the road. I mean, this was Saturday morning, and yet it felt like the whole of Ireland had disappeared and forgot to tell the select few of us. My stop was next, so I pressed the red button to stop the bus, but the bus just kept going straight past it, like the stop wasn't even there.

'Em, why didn't you stop?' I asked the bus man.

The bus braked hard. Suddenly, I went flying into the window.

'Get out here then,' the driver said to me in a harsh tone.

What's his problem? I said to myself as I got off.

Making my way home, I noticed that all the shops were shut.

What is going on today? The only people I saw were a group of what looked like ten-year-olds starting a huge fire. One by one, their small innocent-looking faces turned and looked at me. I started to run. I didn't know what was going on, I just knew I needed to get home and fast.

When I got to my front door I slid my key in to the lock as fast as I could.

'Mam, Dad, I'm home,' I called, but got no answer.

As I walked around my house I heard a thump coming from my little brother's room.

'Andy, are you ok?' I shouted as I ran up the stairs.

Andy was lying on the floor. His eyes were closed and you could hear he was breathing very heavily. He was having one of his fits.

'No, no! Andy, look at me, Andy look at me right now!' I shouted and ran to his side.

He didn't answer. I ran and got the house phone and rang 999. It rang out. How can this be happening? I tried my mam and dad's phones, but no answer from them either.

'OK Andy, if the doctors won't come to us we'll go to them,' I said, trying to get an answer.

I lifted my little brother onto my back and went outside. As I walked down the empty main road I realised I should know what to do if something like this happens. I mean, am I really that lazy?

I got really tired carrying him but I knew I could not stop; he was barely breathing at this stage. Everything that could go wrong seemed to. I looked up and felt the first salty and lukewarm drop of rain soak my face. I wasn't sure where the hospital was and I couldn't carry him for much longer. Then, in the middle of the road, the strain of it all got to me and I dropped Andy to the ground.

When I eventually looked up I saw three people walking towards us. As they came closer I could make out they were: John, my mam and dad. Their gazes were empty and terrifying.

'Look what you have done, Ruairi,' my mam said, but it wasn't her voice, it was a man's one. Then my dad spoke, 'Can't you do anything right?'

It was the same voice as my mam's. The voice was familiar but I couldn't place it.

'It wasn't my fault. I came home and he was on the floor,' I said, hoping that they would stop acting like this and help Andy.

'No Ruairi, you should know how to help him, but that would make you put in an effort, wouldn't it?' John said in a way that made me panic. The voice that they were all speaking in was mine.

'What's happening here?'

This is where I am now.

'What do you think is happening here?' my mam said to me.

'We're just acting like you. Not a care in the world.'

'You think that everyone is against you, so who needs them?' my Dad said in my voice.

'How long is it going to take for you to cop on that there is more to life than resenting people because they try to get your act together?' John said.

'People have told me this for so long, but for the first time I can see what they mean. Look, I swear I'll try my best, OK, just please help Andy, please. I need your help,' I said as I looked down at Andy, tears coming to my eyes.

'You swear?' my mam said.

All three of them started laughing.

'What good is your word?'

'When have you ever kept a promise?'

'I swear on Andy's life.'

The three of them looked at me and all said together,

'We will see.'

I looked up. The smell of the forest floor hit me hard. I jumped up, only to fall right back down, my legs giving way.

I was in the forest. What was all that? I thought to myself. It couldn't have been a dream, could it?

As I walked around the forest thinking of everything that had happened, I felt something had changed in me. But how do I know I'm back in the real world? I got to the road, the bus was on time.

Alex Ó Láighléis is currently based in Dublin, in his parents' house. He enjoys football and reading, but never at the same time. He likes to wake up early as it gives him a chance to reflect in the quiet of the house. He enjoys going to Shay's house on Wednesday, with Stee.

MISSING

Bríd Ní Chomáin

MR DALY

That first day was the hardest. The longest. The worst day in a long time. Phone ringing non-stop. Questions buzzing around my head like some persistent insect. Where did she go? How did this happen? Could I have stopped this? What now? I don't know. I don't know so don't ask me.

I heard she was having trouble with some other students. *I heard* isn't what people want me to say though. They want me to be confident and assured and to know what's going on. I don't though. I do really feel for that poor girl's family. Holly's family. That was her name: Holly. Jesus, I hope it's still her name.

It's awful to admit but I didn't recognise the girl at first. Her sister is in first year; didn't recognise her either. But it's quite a big school and other than a few problems in second year, Holly had never caused any real trouble. And even then she was just another kid becoming a teenager. You know the sort; girls wear too much makeup, boys fight. They 'forget' their homework a lot and they stare at you blankly, as if you haven't been teaching for fifteen years.

This being my first year as principal, I took the tough-guy approach.

You don't mess with Gordon Daly.

—Do you have anything important to be doing?

—No, sir.

—Wonderful. Get to class.

I'd thought I was doing well. Respected and feared. I'd also thought I was getting to know the students on a brand-new level. Obviously not all of them.

But I know lots of my students.

I know some of their mothers from the committee. Or I know them through sport, or academic achievements. Or they have a learning difficulty and I talk to them from time to time. Or they cause trouble because of what's going on in their lives. Or they cause trouble because they're just bold.

Holly Keyes was none of these things. But that doesn't mean that she's not a part of the school. It doesn't mean that if she was struggling she didn't deserve help.

Isn't it my job to keep the kids safe? Now one of them is missing. That's a child that I've let down.

What does this mean for that poor girl and her family? For my school?

How did this happen?

NESSA

When she first went missing it was like the whole world stopped spinning.

All normal routine ceased and mam started leaving things in weird places. Her keys in the fridge, pictures of us on holiday in Clare stuffed down the side of the couch. Nobody said anything because we knew she wasn't herself.

No one was themselves without Holly around to tell us we were doing it wrong.

It started almost immediately, the family cracking up. In the first couple of days dad began staying up in the office all day and night, leaving mam to flit around the house, acting like a 1960s housewife.

I just stopped. Talking, smiling. Thinking.

One of those evenings mam came in and busied herself making dinner. All the pots and pans banging around in the kitchen. Singing to herself like nothing was different. Like nothing was missing. Like there wasn't a gaping hole in our lives the size of the entire Milky Way.

At around half six she walked into the front room and found me still sitting in the dark. She seemed most put-out that I'd left the curtains open, letting the whole world into our little prison.

—What're you doing sitting in the dark, love?

A nervous laugh.

Mam's eyes stared out at me from over two purple bruises. I knew she wasn't sleeping. I'd heard her bustling around downstairs in the small hours of the night, working on missing person posters, emailing newspapers and radio stations.

My sister was gone just four days and mam had already made it the only thing that mattered.

I'd always thought she was a bit of a nutcase, my mam. Like she couldn't let anything go. When she and I fought, which wasn't often, she won. Always.

Mam and Holly were both like that.

There's something about loving people – family, like, that makes you miss the bad things just as much as the good. More. I noticed that when Holly disappeared.

Apart from worrying that my sister was dead in a ditch or being held captive by terrorists or something, the only thing that really bothered me when she was gone was how quiet everything was. God knows I didn't have much to say for myself.

Holly was always the loud one. She was sarcastic and chatty and everyone loved her. I stayed in the corner and smiled politely and said please and thank you.

Holly found it most entertaining.

—One day, when you're older, someone is going to drunkenly punch you and you're going to apologise for putting your face in front of their fist and then ask is their hand OK.

Sometimes I felt like Holly only lived to mock me for being a 'good girl'.

But that was only on her worst days, the rest of the time she acted like I was the smartest person on the planet, like I could be president if I wanted. I knew she thought I was cleverer than her. We used to watch TV quiz shows together and she'd always say to me,

—You knew that one didn't you?

She said it no matter what the question was and I always said yeah. Just for the laugh.

Because me and Holly laughing together was the best thing in the world.

You know when you're younger and you go on family outings and by the end of the day you are so tired that you just curl up in the backseat and fall asleep? And when you go to parties as a kid and you run around screaming and eat so much cake you burst and get sick everywhere but you don't even care? And when you're five and it's summer and your parents break out the paddling pool and it's the absolute best day ever?

Sometimes when I look back on days like that it makes me kind of sad, because I know that nothing will ever really be that simple again.

But me and Holly laughing was like that.

About a week after Holly went missing my English teacher had us write a paragraph about a great holiday, and bring in a picture to match. My picture was one of me and Holly sitting on a big cannon at some eighteenth-century castle and Holly is falling straight off. Both our faces are priceless. Me smiling like a lunatic and Holly flying towards the ground, looking like the world just exploded.

In the end I didn't give up the photo. I just kept it in my pocket, carried it around school for a couple of days.

Every classroom I went into I felt like I was invading Holly's personal space. Like every chair I sat on I was pushing Holly out of it. I walked down the hallway and everyone looked at me.

—That's Holly Keyes's little sister. Yeah, Holly Keyes that's gone missing.

Holly was always the one people talked about. It felt strange that with her gone there was only me left to point at.

I'd noticed that she'd stopped coming to school. I felt it was my duty as her little sister not to say anything. Be cool.

The day she went missing I saw her get up in the morning, pretend to get ready. I didn't see her all day and I was finally going to say something about her playing truant when I got home.

But she wasn't there. And she didn't come back.

On the day the note came, I was so worried that I should have said something sooner. That something had been really wrong and she'd been attacked over some sort of school trouble.

The awful stories you hear.

So when I let myself in and saw it stuffed in the letterbox I didn't know who it could be from. Didn't know what it would tell me. Or what was going on.

Sometimes I wish that note had never come.

I could go on just missing Holly. And not hating her.

AVA

She got on at Harts Corner. Stumbled with a huge bag on the last few steps, glanced down the narrow walkway and found me sitting on one of the back seats.

Her face emptied of emotion. It was scary, like, the way she looked through me, looked past my half smile.

She probably knew, anyway. Knew it was me who helped

those rumours along on their path of destruction. I felt honest remorse. I did, swear.

All my friends said she brought it on herself.

What could I do, anyway?

Holly never did anything really bad – apart from deciding she was going to be a slut after Mags O'Connor moved away, but I guess she was lonely.

I'd always kinda liked her; liked the idea of being friends with Mags and Holly, that double act from the year above. But, honestly, who was actually friends with either of them? With Mags gone everyone realised that all we really knew about them were things like Holly couldn't hold her drink and Mags could, which songs they'd dance to, where they bought their clothes.

So Holly still got invited everywhere, still used those sarcastic lines and got a laugh but she ended up standing alone at most parties.

The perfect prey for drunken boys.

I don't know who started the rumours, really. It was a combined effort of the female population at school.

—Holly Keyes was meeting Darren Dunne in a bush at his sisters eighteenth. Slut.

—Holly Keyes said she'd take someone's ex-fella after a week. Bitch.

—Everyone knows Holly Keyes was with Robbie Byrne at some party last week. She's not even *trying* to keep it quiet. Skank.

Once the girls around me got wind of Holly's indiscretions it spread like wild fire. And it's partly Holly's fault 'cause she's a naturally open person.

I think with Mags gone she got a bit mixed up about who to trust and who to avoid like the plague when it came to secret-keeping.

She trusted people who only wanted to see her go down.

Did she trust me?

I looked back at her as I headed for the bus stairs, just

once, to offer some sort of apology. But her stare caught me off guard and I retreated.

Retreated to the world of my friends and the comfort of another Z-list celebrity book signing.

Later, in the Jervis Centre bathrooms, I stood next to Lisa, mascara tube in hand and told her about seeing Holly.

—It's not like she has any reasons to mitch school.

She laughed outright. Ended the conversation like that.

—We're gonna have to get a move-on if we wanna get there before the rest of the sluts . . . Holly Keyes isn't going, is she?

That laugh again. Cold, callous. I answered with my own. Forced. And I swear I could feel her, Holly, standing there, staring right through me.

How could I have known?

CARL

From where I sat I had a good view of the street. I watched a fella in a grey suit trekking towards me through the snow. He dodged a puddle of sick on the path, stepped in my direction.

I stuck out me coffee cup.

'Anything small to spare?'

He laughed in me face and kept walking. I reached over and picked up a can. Threw it after the creep.

I heard her laughing before I saw her. Didn't know her – and she was just standing there laughing at me. If she'd been a boy, I would've given her such a deck.

'What are *you* laughin' at?'

I pulled me hood tighter round me face, turned away, but she didn't leave.

'Is there somethin' I can do for ye?'

'Are you homeless?'

'Yeah I'm homeless. D'ye tink I'm just sittin' here 'cause I like snow in me jocks?'

'Well, *sorry*. I've been walking around for about an hour 'cause I lost my phone. You're from Dublin. Can I sit with you?'

As if me being from Dublin meant we were going to be friends or something. But I took a glance at her. Her jeans were soaked through and she'd two suitcases and her shoulder bag seemed like it weighed a ton. She looked wrecked and desperate.

'If you've nothin' better to do.'

She'd nothing better to do.

She took out a small box of Crunchy Nut Cornflakes, out of one of them variety packs. I know that doesn't sound like much but I didn't eat that day and I would've taken anything. She put it straight in me hands.

We sat in silence for a bit.

Her phone rang. She hung up quickly but not before I saw the word 'Mam' on the screen.

'What's your name?

She looked up, relieved, I think.

'Holly.'

'I'm Carl.'

She nodded. I think she was giving me the choice of starting a conversation.

'How did you end up here?'

And it was like that was the question she'd been waiting years for someone to ask her. She told me about herself. And I got the feeling what she was telling me were things she'd never even said out loud before. About the girls at her school and a bunch of stories they spread; some of them true, some of them just blatant lies.

And about her little sister being a genius. And her best friend moving away. And school being too hard. And the rumours, the rumours, the rumours.

'Did ye not have any other friends to stick up for ye?'

I never know what to say when people are telling me serious stories. It's another thing that used to drive me ma mental. Another reason I ended up living here with me da. Which turned out to be a not-so-great idea.

Anyways her eyes got all wide like a little puppy. And she started crying.

I can't handle it when girls cry.

I couldn't think of anything to say that didn't make me sound like a gobshite. So I patted her on the back a bit and changed the subject.

And she stayed sitting with me for the day. And I told her about meself. And some of the things I told her were things I had never said out loud before.

About me ma and me da and all their problems. And how I used to leave home for days at a time. And nobody ever noticed.

It was weird, like, saying all that to some girl I didn't know. But I felt like we were in the same situation.

Just before it started getting dark she took out a map and an address scribbled on a piece of paper. It kinda hit me then that she had it so much better.

She had somewhere to go.

I helped her find her friend's house on the map. She started packing up her little shoulder bag and I couldn't think of anything I could do that would stop her.

I stood up to say goodbye.

There was a question I was burning to ask her though, a part of the story that I couldn't wrap me head around.

'What about your Leavin' Cert?'

This made her stop packing. She stopped moving and just stared.

'Well I'm not going to do it.'

'Oh, righ' . . . but you could?'

'Well . . . yeah. But I don't even know what I want to be, so what's the point in going through all that pressure for nothing?'

'Hardly for nothing. Like, you have the chance?'

'Yeah. But I don't want it.'

'You don't want a job and a house?'

'I can still get all that without the Leaving.'

'Oh, righ', yeah course ye can.'

'What kind of life would that be anyway? Wasting my time studying and getting some stuck-up job I hate just so I can have a house?'

'But?'

'But nothing. You don't even get it.'

I looked at her.

Her stupid face. Her Abercrombie & Fitch hoody and her jeans without a rip or a stain in sight. Brand new runners, suitcases of stuff, rucksack on one shoulder full of the kind of things rich people think us homeless peasants need.

She was the one who didn't get it.

'But some of us aren't that lucky! Some of us get no chance and there you are, could do whatever you wanted to and you're just not arsed?! That's the biggest load of bull!'

'You don't know what it's like! I had to!'

'*You* don't know what it's like! Livin' on street corners. You're lucky, you've got a home all set up for ye. All cosy. Good luck to ye. People like you never learn from their mistakes. They get everythin' handed to them on a silver platter.'

She was crying again. I didn't even care.

I was so angry and I didn't even know why.

'I hope you have a very nice life Holly. Maybe I'll see ye again. I'm not goin' anywhere am I?'

She grabbed her bags, turned away from me.

The tears streaming down her face, she started walking away.

'You know what, Carl? It's not my fault you ended up like this.'

'IT'S NOT MY FAULT EITHER!'

I watched her blunder off down the road, dragging the suitcases after her. Coughing and crying and falling over her own feet. There was this urge in me to run after her. Stop her and just make her listen, make her see the chances she was throwing away. But I knew she'd learn soon enough, so I just stared after her.

I didn't know what would happen to her. Or me.

After a minute she turned a corner and was gone. Most of me hoped she found her friend's house straightaway. Get off the streets, away from anything bad.

Back to the perfect life she was used to.

A small part of me thought she deserved to wander around for a while. Sleep in a doorway, wake up freezing and understand what she was giving up.

Only a small part, though.

I sat back down on my cardboard box.

HOLLY

Nessa,

I wish I could give you a solid reason for all the trouble I've caused. But honestly, I don't have one. It just seemed like with Mags gone I had to prove that I was worth talking to. And I got really tired.

I'm sorry I made you all worry. I'm safe.

Holly x

This story appeared as 'Truant' in the 'Fighting Words – New Young Voices in Irish Writing' supplement in *The Irish Times* **on 13 April 2011.**

 **Bríd Ní Chomáin is fifteen. She lives with her Mam, Dad and brother in Finglas. Bríd likes talking. If anyone likes talking, it's Bríd. Talking is her favourite thing to do. She likes writing – but she likes talking more.**

THE FALLEN IRISH

Cameron Ó Fiannaí

As dawn approached on a summer's day in August 1960, I, CPL Joseph Fitzgerald, arrived in the Democratic Republic of Congo. I was part of a UN Force to aid the newly-formed Democratic Republic to maintain its territorial integrity. Assigned to the 32nd battalion led by Lt Col Nut Buckley, it was our job to keep the peace. As I stepped off the truck I knew I wasn't in Dublin anymore. The climate wasn't doing me any favours. Sweat dripping from my forehead, sun hot on my shoulders, my t-shirt was sticking to me and I knew, with my red hair, I'd find it difficult to acclimatise.

'Belter of a day isn't it Joe?' said Smithy. Smithy was a great friend of mine. We'd known each other for many years through the army. This was our first big 'mission' since joining the army and my nerves were getting the better of me. I took my pack from the back of the truck and headed for the main hall in the camp with the rest of the guys.

'Good morning gentlemen,' said Sgt McSweeney, a small, bald aggressive Irish man. 'Here is where you'll stay.' He turned and walked away, leaving us to settle in.

*

The next morning we were awoken abruptly by Sgt Max Oaksy. 'Rise and shine, ladies. Lieutenant Buckley wants to see you. Today eleven of you will be patrolling a bridge over the Luweyeye River in the town of Niemba.'

'You ready for this?' I asked Smithy as we followed Sgt Oaksy down to the truck. Privately, I knew I wasn't. We hopped into the back of the truck with our Lee Enfield rifles on our backs. After an hour-long journey along the Luweyeye River we arrived at the bridge. Sgt Oaksy laid a map of the area on top of the bonnet of the truck and showed us were we would be patrolling. The midday sun beamed down on our heavy uniforms as we started to march. After a while conversation dropped and every little sound could be heard. The day seemed endless. Suddenly we heard screams coming from every direction. 'Hear that?' I asked Smithy. Oaksy began to yell.

'We're under Attack! We're under attack!'

Panic kicked in. We took our rifles from our backs and headed for the bridge. My heart was pumping. We took cover at one end of the bridge behind a tree. 'Stand your ground! Stand your ground!' Oaksy kept repeating. They came in their hundreds, Baluba tribesmen racing down the muddy road with poison-tipped arrows. 'Ready. Aim. Fire!' yelled Oaksy. I cocked my rifle and began shooting. They dropped like flies at first, but advanced steadily until we were outnumbered and our troops were the ones beginning to fall. Blood everywhere and men who I'd spent years with in the army were lying face-down in the dirt. We were surrounded, down to the last three. Myself, Sgt Oaksy and Smithy.

Oaksy grabbed me by the shoulder and nodded at the river. I put my rifle on my back, took a deep breath, counted to three and ran as fast I could over the bridge; the whistling noise of the bullets passing my ears as we jumped. A noise, a clatter, as the three of us hit the water hard.

'Where's Oaksy?' I screamed at Smithy, who had surfaced beside me.

'Oaksy! Oaksy!' we yelled. Suddenly we saw him, floating face-down, blood seeping from a wound. Our first day. Every man dead, except Smithy and I.

*

We headed south, in search of the nearest base camp, fearful that the tribe might follow. By the end of the day, we had covered twenty kilometres and there was no sign of the tribe, but no sign of the base camp either.

'Better set up for the night,' I said to Smithy. I don't think I'd slept a minute, when the noises began. Tooting, whistling, it was the enemy communicating with each other. The night was long and cold and I didn't sleep at all. Morning came and we were both starving. No food and morale was low.

'Joe! Look!' Smithy whispered. I turned my head and watched the bushes shake. From nowhere, an arrow whizzed by.

'Hit the deck!' I ordered. I fired a shot into the bush and a loud scream could be heard.

A tribesman for the Baluba tribe lay motionless on the ground. Was he still alive? I wondered. I gave him a little kick to look for signs of life and noticed his eyes flicker. Smithy ran over and started kicking him hard in the side.

'Finish him,' he shouted at me. I stood in front of the boy. He was no more than fifteen, fear in his eyes, sweat dripping from his head. He began begging for mercy. 'What you waiting for! Do it Joe! Blow his head off!' Smithy shouted. With the rifle still in my hands I slowly raised it and put my index finger on the trigger. My stomach was churning and I felt physically sick. 'Do it!' Smithy shouted. Everything around me fell still. I looked at the wounded boy.

'I can't!' I shouted at Smithy. 'I can't. I didn't sign up for this.' I let the gun slide from my hand and fell to my knees.

'Fine, I'll kill him myself,' Smithy said. He reached into his jacket, pulled out a small pistol and walked over to the boy.

He put his mud-soiled boot on the boy's chest, raised his gun in line with his head and took aim. I jumped up and stood in front of Smithy.

'No!' I shouted. 'We're here to keep the peace. We're not murderers.' Smithy wrestled with me for a second, punching and kicking. 'He's only a kid!' I shouted.

'He's a kid that tried to kill you,' Smithy shouted back. 'You're mad,' he shook his head. I took some rope from my bag, tied the kid's hands together and we set off. After hours of walking we came to a river. This was the ideal opportunity to get food but we'd no fishing equipment or bait.

'Maybe the boy knows how,' I said to Smithy. 'Tribes hunt for fish all the time.' Smithy walked over to the boy and asked could he catch us some fish but the boy didn't understand. Smithy tried hand signals. It worked. The boy nodded his head, walked over to a tree and pointed towards a branch. We realised he wanted us to cut it down and sharpen it for him.

'I'm not sure about this,' said Smithy. Nor was I, but he was our only chance for food so we gave the boy the sharpened stick. He stood at the edge of the river for fifteen minutes, then he struck the harpoon-shaped stick into the water and speared a large fish. 'Food!' Smithy shouted.

'Start a fire,' I said. Food never tasted so good. I ate every bit of fish off those bones. We all did. Night fell, and we put a gag on the prisoner's mouth to stop him shouting for the tribesmen if they came back during the night. I stayed awake for ages but eventually fell asleep. Frantic sounds woke me in the morning as the prisoner, wild-eyed beneath the gag, writhed and struggled, his eyes fixed on something moving quickly through the grass.

It was a Tree Viper, a highly venomous snake.

'Damn!' Smithy shouted. 'I've been bitten!' Our prisoner was struggling to get free. He shouted words at us that we didn't understand, but I knew he wanted to help. By now

Smithy was sweating like a pig and gasping for air. I took a knife from my belt and cut the rope from our prisoner's hand. He looked at me for a minute, then turned and ran into the jungle, never to be seen again. Or so I thought.

*

Smithy got worse and there was nothing I could do. I braced myself for the fact that I was about to lose my best friend, that I was about to be left alone in this place, possibly to die myself. It seemed like an hour had passed, then, to my surprise, our prisoner returned, carrying berries in his hand. He mixed the berries with leaves and water and made some sort of potion. He lifted Smithy's head and helped him to drink it.

'You're gonna be alright Smithy,' I said, not knowing if he really would be.

It was now a race against time as we set off to find the base camp, where I knew there would be a medical team. I took Smithy under one arm and the prisoner took the other. Smithy's legs trailed as we carried him, and every ten minutes or so we had to stop to rest. For a young boy, the prisoner had great endurance and why he helped us, I will never know. We made our way as fast as we could through the jungle with our prisoner leading the way. At one point, I don't know why, I began to doubt him. Was he leading us towards the tribesmen? I gripped my rifle. Two hours later we were still half-walking, half-dragging a worsening Smithy.

'Stay with me Smithy,' I said. Smithy was hallucinating now, and getting sick and his chances of survival looked slim. I felt terrible. Completely exhausted. I didn't know if I could go on much longer. Suddenly, up ahead, a light in the distance, faint at first, then brighter. It was an opening. 'Come on!' I shouted at our prisoner, and we picked up our pace.

'This is it Smithy,' I said, jogging towards the light. 'This is it.' And then I saw it. A glimmer of red through the trees. I squinted and stared again. It was a cross. A large red cross. The Base Camp Hospital. Happiness shot through my body and I felt heat in my face as I pushed the tears away. Beside me, I watched our prisoner lay Smithy gently on the ground. He looked at me, then stood back. I looked at the boy and nodded. A nod of thanks. A nod of acceptance, because I knew what he was going to do. I watched him turn and walk away. I didn't try to stop him.

Cameron Ó Fiannaí is sixteen and was born in Dublin. He lives with his Mam, Dad and sister. He loves playing football and his favourite team is Liverpool. He also enjoys playing golf. He hates spiders and an empty fridge.

DOMESTIC BLISS

Caoimhe Ní Mhúineacháin

I looked at my watch. The last hour had seemed to fly by in a minute. I was late for my very important camogie match and I just knew Brian was going to kill me.

I joined camogie a few years ago to get out of the house and out of my Mam's way. I remember being really nervous before my first match but excited as though my stomach was spinning inside me. I don't know why I was afraid, because everyone made me feel so welcome and Liam the manager was great. He really helped me learn all I needed to know. Then one day Liam left because he had got a new job in England and Brian took over. That's when my love for camogie started to fade.

'Mam, Mam I need a lift to camogie, I'm late. Mam! Will you hurry up?'

'For God's sake Emily, you can't keep doing this every time camogie is on, I'm getting really sick of it.'

'Okay, Mam, I'm sorry, but can you just please get a move on. I'm in enough trouble with Brian as it is.'

'Well Brian will have to wait a few minutes until I'm finished watching *Loose Women*. Sometimes I wish you cared as much about me as you do about Brian.'

'Are you crazy? I couldn't care less about Brian. I want to be on time because he scares the crap out of me and I could lose my place on the team. So please can you get your ass off the couch and let's go!'

'Excuse me, what makes you think you can speak to me like that? If you don't want to walk to your match I'd suggest you watch your tone.'

'Alright, alright, I didn't mean it Mam.'

The drive to the match seemed to take forever. I couldn't stop looking at the clock. I was itching to get there so I wouldn't be in more trouble then I already was.

'Hey Mam, are you going to stay and watch my match and then we can give a few of the girls a lift home?' She let out a snigger. Mam always made it quite clear she had no interest in my camogie.

'Of course not Emily, you know well and good Mark has his football matches every Saturday and he would be completely gutted if I missed them.'

I don't know why I bothered asking. I knew already what the answer would be, but I had hoped I would be wrong.

*

I could hear Mam banging around downstairs and I knew it was going to be a long night, just like every Friday.

'Mark, Emily, dinner's ready.'

Silence filled the hallway.

'Emily! Get down here now.'

'Mam I was finishing my homework,' I shouted from my bedroom.

'Well that doesn't give you an excuse to ignore me and to ignore the fact that I slaved over this dinner for you and your brother.'

As I came down the stairs, Mark strolled out of the living room, the theme tune of *Scrubs* following behind him.

'Mam, did you not just see Mark come out of there, doing

nothing while you shouted at me for not answering . . . I was doing homework!'

Mark smirked and I just knew inside his head he was applauding himself.

'Emily, I'm not in the mood! Making this dinner has drained all my energy.'

'Yeah, grilled chicken and frozen chips for God's sake, how draining can that be?'

Mam shot me a glare as she heard me mutter to myself.

'Mark, take over the salt and Emily you wait here so you can take over the juice and the plates when I'm finished dishing out the food.'

I couldn't even speak I was so frustrated. It was the same all the time. Mark got the easy job and I was stuck doing everything else.

This was usually Dad's cue to walk in. When all the work was done and all he had to do was sit down, eat, give out and then retreat to the study. But today he was late.

'Mam, can we just start eating without Dad? Put his plate in the oven, it'll be grand.'

'Emily, we never eat without your father, where is he?'

'Mam c'mon, we're starving and anyway it's his problem if he's late, not ours. He knows what time dinner is at,' said Mark.

'I'm sorry Mark, but I can't help it if I'm worried about your father, you know he drives like a lunatic.'

It's not like he ever worries about any of us anyway, I thought.

'Right, well I suppose we may as well eat, so my cooking doesn't go to waste.'

We ate in silence, everyone occupied by their own thoughts, when Dad pushed through the door creating a lot of noise and snapping everyone back to reality.

'Oh, Peter, where have you been? You know dinner is at six and you're twenty minutes late.'

'Kate, just give it a rest for crying out loud. I'm only in the door and you're nagging me.'

'Well Peter I'm sorry if my so-called "nagging" annoys you,' Mam said, slamming back her chair. Dad lowered himself into his usual place at the head of the table, while Mam flung the oven door open.

'Kate, will you go easy with that thing. It wasn't free, you know.'

She dropped the hot plate sending food all over the place, before bursting into tears. I glanced at Mark and we both slipped out of the kitchen into the sitting room. They were now screaming at each other.

'I'm going out,' Mark said with no hint of emotion in his voice.

'What? You can't leave me here with them, like that.'

'Watch this then,' Mark called over his shoulder as he slammed the front door behind him.

Even though he was seventeen, Mark never handled the fights well. He always went out for ages, ended up coming home drunk, with mam trying to get him to bed before dad noticed. Not that dad cared about anything in the house.

I dragged myself up the stairs to my bedroom to try and get away from the racket. It was the same all the time. Sometimes I wondered which was worse, Mam's unsupportive, unenthusiastic attitude towards everything, or dad just not getting involved. It just seemed that I didn't belong in this family. Mark fit in alright, but I didn't!

I must have dozed off, because next thing I know mam and dad were standing in the doorway, both wearing their dressing gowns. A drunken Mark was holding himself up against the wall, a greenish tint to his face.

'What time do you call this, Mark?' Mam said.

Mark didn't answer as he staggered off to the bathroom, his hands over his mouth. He's in some amount of trouble now, I thought.

'Emily, do you know Mark has just been taken home in a squad car for the third time this month?'

'Ohh right, but why are you shouting this at me Mam?'

'I'm just worried, Emily.'

'He better not lose his scholarship to the Australian Institute of Sport, now that he has a record,' Dad shouted at me.

'O . . . kay.'

Next thing Mam exploded at me.

'Well I hope you're happy now! I can't believe you let him go out, if he doesn't get to go to Australia it should be on your conscience for ever!'

'WHAT?'

I sat there, my mouth gaping, lost for words.

Caoimhe Ní Mhúineacháin is sixteen years old, was born in Northern Ireland and moved to Dublin when she was two. She now lives in Beaumont with her Mam, Dad, and three younger sisters. She plays piano, has a cat called Pebbles, enjoys music and dislikes snakes.

CHRONOSHIFT

Ciarán Ó Duibhghinn

Monday. Calvin Buchanan was headed for platform 2. His neatly polished loafers squeaked loudly, pestering their owner to slacken the pace. Calvin hopped into the nearest railcar. The doors sealed silently behind him. Using the window as a mirror, he flattened his windblown hair down and straightened his tie. He took a seat by one of the tables, cradling his daily planner notebook in his hand.

Just another Monday. Dark, bleak and depressing. Calvin had a meeting at 9:45 am. He glanced at his watch. He had fifteen minutes to show up, and he was on his last warning. Calvin was new to this job and had already been given his fair share of second chances. The train finally began to roll. Calvin reached inside his jacket and took out his iPod.

'Nothing like some soothing music to calm the nerves,' Calvin mumbled to himself. He looked out into the morning. The trees were layered in frost and a peculiar fog hung ghost-like in the air, blocking out the beautiful mountains that surrounded the city. Calvin spotted small rabbits in the undergrowth as the train trundled through the silence of land left untouched by the land developers.

All too soon for Calvin, the train wheels screeched to a halt. Surrounding him was a concrete jungle. Tall buildings shut out the sky and the strong smell of pollution clouded the air. He headed straight for his office that was opposite the train station. Shuffling through the mob of businessmen and - women was a task in itself that Calvin had become accustomed to. Then, Calvin saw the strangest sight. A man dressed in black was running through the crowd with a pink handbag, while a Chihuahua was nipping at his heels. Distracted, Calvin was instantly bowled over to the ground by the crowds of people.

'Hey, watch where you're going!' Calvin roared, but his voice was lost in the hustle and bustle that was the morning commute. Suddenly, he panicked. His hands were empty. He sprang up, and scanned the ground for it.

'Where is it!?' Calvin's heart skipped a beat.

The planner that he needed so vitally for his meeting was lost in the crowd. He had no time and he decided to make do without it and instead recite his presentation from memory, and so he rushed to work. He wagered that it would be better to go on to the meeting than waste his time looking for the planner in the crowd. He just couldn't be late for the meeting. Being on time was of the utmost importance where Calvin worked, and today more so than ever.

Two minutes later, Calvin was running towards the closing lift. He pushed button number 13 which started to glow . . . 1, 2, 3 . . . Calvin checked his watch. He had three minutes. He was going to make it. Or so he thought. Midway between floors 9 and 10, the numbers stopped changing and the lights flickered out. The lift made a grinding sound as it shuddered to a standstill. Calvin stared into the darkness dumbly.

'No. This can't be happening,' he stammered. 'Not today, please!'

Minutes ticked away. After a delay, Calvin whipped out his Nokia and dialled the number for the receptionist on the ground floor.

'Hello, Debbie speaking, how may I help you?'

'Receptionist lady? It's me Calvin!'

'My name is Debbie,' was the blunt reply.

'Yeah, sure, listen, I'm stuck in lift number two somewhere between floor 9 and 10, can you get someone up here to fix it ASAP?'

'Hmm, I guess I have to considering I might lose my job if I don't. Especially because I'm not as qualified as all you people that work in offices. No, I just answer the phone and tell people they have the wrong number.'

'Please, stop rambling and get someone to fix the lift.'

The phone beeped in his hand. More minutes passed and Calvin started to lose control of his emotions. Tears started rolling down his cheeks. He hadn't even realised that the lift had already restarted its ascent. But it didn't matter anymore, he had missed the meeting. Suddenly, light flooded the lift. Calvin shielded his eyes and then saw the unmistakable outline of his boss, Harry Ustinov. The sight of Ustinov's tank-like frame and shiny, slick black hair was enough for Calvin to conjure the image of a hammer and sickle flag fluttering behind him. Especially now, after missing his presentation, this was the last person he wanted to see. There was a deafening silence between the two men. Calvin rose up from his knees and wiped his face.

'Just looking for my keys,' he stuttered nervously. 'Found them.'

Calvin walked quickly past Ustinov, avoiding eye contact. He unlocked his office and slammed the door behind him. He slumped into his chair. He had missed his presentation and made a fool of himself in front of Harry Ustinov. Calvin could already picture all of his managers in the boardroom downstairs packing up their briefcases in disgust, thinking 'This idiot Calvin has had so many chances, he's really blown it this time. Wait 'til Ustinov hears about this!'

Calvin detected a rhythmic glowing in the corner of his

eye. He turned around and saw his computer screen. He pushed himself towards it and a window of Solitaire opened up. 'You lose,' was the message displayed, mocking him. Calvin sighed heavily.

The remainder of the day dragged on slowly. Calvin couldn't bear to leave his office. No way. He was simply too ashamed to show his face. He couldn't bear confronting his colleagues or worse, bumping into Ustinov in the corridors.

*

At long last, Calvin was back home in his apartment and somewhat relieved. He popped a meal into the microwave and trudged towards the bedroom. A sudden, shrill ringing pierced his eardrums. He held onto the wall. It was just his phone, ringing in his pocket. He answered when he realised that whoever it was wasn't going to leave him alone.

'Hello, who is it?' Calvin asked suspiciously.

'Calvin Buchanan!' It was the unmistakable voice of Harry Ustinov.

'Oh, Mr Ustinov!' Calvin laughed uneasily 'How nice to hear from you.'

'Well, Mr Buchanan, a little bird just told me that you never turned up for your presentation at ten o'clock this morning.' His tone changed. 'Why?'

'I was stuck in the lift,' Calvin mumbled. 'I was rushing to my presentation when the lift stopped moving'

A deep chuckle boomed into Calvin's ear.

'What is it?' Calvin asked.

'You absolute fool. I let you take this presentation because I believed you could do the job!' Harry shouted. A silence hung over the line. 'Listen here Calvin, I've put my neck on the line for you enough times already and you haven't changed your ways. I'm not seeing any results and you're just not up to scratch. For that reason, I'm going to let you go. Come in tomorrow to sign the papers and make this official.'

The line went dead. Calvin felt the anger boiling up inside him.

'How could they do this to me! It wasn't my fault! Well, not today anyway.'

He slammed the phone down and sighed heavily.

*

Ustinov's voice rang in Calvin's ears for the rest of the evening, which dragged on slowly. Eventually, Calvin reached his bed and he slipped under the duvet and drifted into a sad and lonely world.

*

Calvin strained an eye open and reached out for his alarm clock. The muscles in his arm were screaming at him. He rubbed his eyes wearily. The whole room spun around him, everything blurry. After his eyes had adjusted, he twisted out of the comfort of his bed. His legs felt like they'd been injected with concrete. He shuffled awkwardly to the bathroom, where he instantly collapsed on the floor. Calvin used the sink to lever himself up again. He cleaned the mist off the mirror and examined himself. He was too dizzy to see anything. He felt his legs give way again, so he held the sink to support himself. Calvin closed his eyes. What's happening to me? he thought. All the strength in his body started slipping away and his mind went blank.

A black sea enveloped Calvin. Colourful patterns floated into view, just drifting on by. Time passed slowly here, sometimes as if it was standing still. Suddenly, there was a rush of energy and Calvin snapped awake. His phone was ringing. He saw the Nokia flashing on his bedside drawer. He immediately remembered collapsing at the sink the night before and wondered how he got back in bed. He looked at the phone.

1 new voice message from H.Ustinov

'What does he want now? I'll sign the papers when I feel like it.'

He pressed the *listen* button. 'Calvin, comrade, I just wanted to wish you good luck with that presentation today. No pressure, but it's a very big deal to us. I trust you'll do the job well.'

Silence. Calvin walked over to the window. Grey clouds blocked up the sky and another peculiar fog was hanging ghost-like in the air. He dropped his phone and walked out the door of his apartment. He saw the old man from across the hall unlocking his door. Calvin rushed over to him. 'Mr Buchanan, how nice to see you. Umm, where are your clothes?'

'Oh, I'm only awake,' Calvin replied. 'Claude, what day is it today?'

'Hmm, let me see, I had a visit from my grand-daughter yesterday, so today must be Monday.'

The old man smiled at Calvin. Calvin was unsure about Claude's judgment. 'Thanks, Claude.'

Calvin went back into his apartment and shut the door. He lifted his briefcase onto the bed and opened it. Sticking out of it was what looked like the planner notebook he lost at the station just yesterday. He flicked through it and, sure enough, he found his presentation notes. He glanced at the clock. It was twenty past eight.

'How is this happening?' he asked himself. 'What if I really still have my meeting at ten o'clock?' Calvin wondered.

He decided to put on his suit and leave for work as usual. He still had to collect his belongings anyway. En route to the station he picked up the *Free Newport Metro*. The date read Monday, 7th January. His neatly polished shoes were squeaking at him again. Calvin got into the nearest railcar. He took a seat, feeling confused. He opened his briefcase and took out his planner. All his notes were in order.

The following ten minutes consisted of Calvin pacing up

and down the empty carriage, rehearsing. Reading his notes out loud. Testing his tone of voice. He didn't know why he was being given a second chance but he didn't care. He had to get this presentation right. He gathered himself just as the train screeched to a halt. Calvin decisively put his planner back into his briefcase and stepped off the train. It was madness again at the station. Waves of people coming off the train. Waves trying to get on. Both pushing against each other. Calvin heard snarling and spotted the same Chihuahua chasing after the same thief with the pink handbag he had seen before. This time, Calvin headed around the long way to exit the train station to avoid the massive throngs of people. He crossed the road and entered his workplace.

'I think I'll take the stairs this morning,' Calvin grinned to himself.

It was only ten to nine. After climbing thirteen flights of stairs, he still felt optimistic about the day ahead. He went into his office and began reading over his notes again. Then, there was a sharp knock at the door. Calvin looked through his office window. It was Harry. He answered the door and let him in.

'Calvin, I gather you received my message earlier. I know we've had our ups and downs, but I have a good feeling about letting you do this presentation. Please don't let me down.'

'I wouldn't dream of it,' Calvin replied brightly.

'Good to see you in early to read over your notes,' said Harry.

Then he gave what Calvin could only imagine to be a smile. Harry closed the door and left.

Calvin went over his notes again. At five to ten he left his office and made off to the conference room on the same floor. Already, he could see men and women sitting down, each and every one looked professional. Clean suits, fresh faces. Calvin guessed there were about twenty people in there. Waiting for his presentation. He took a deep breath and entered the room.

'Good morning everyone. Is everyone present and ready to begin?'

Calvin sensed that his arrival had changed the atmosphere in the room.

'Yes we're all here,' replied a small woman sitting at the bottom of the long table that dominated the room.

Calvin walked up to the top of the table. He felt confident. The chattering died down as Calvin took centre stage. Calvin composed himself a final time, and began the best presentation of his life.

*

'Well, Calvin, I heard your presentation went brilliantly! In fact, I was told by one of the very people you gave your presentation to that it was a real eye-opener and that I should be proud to have you working with us.'

Calvin smiled awkwardly. It felt strange to hear anything positive about him coming from Harry's mouth.

'Tomorrow, Calvin, take the day off. You've done a lot of work lately and you deserve a break.'

'Thank you, sir! Thank you very much,' replied Calvin enthusiastically.

'It's getting late. You should be on your way home.'

'Yes of course.' Calvin wrapped his scarf loosely around his neck and put on his jacket.

He locked his office behind him, picked up his briefcase and headed off home.

On the train, Calvin felt tired. The trundling wheels almost lulled him to sleep. He began to wonder what happened to him. Had he been dreaming? Why did he wake up feeling so sick this morning? Calvin decided he'd go to the library to do some thinking the next morning. For now, he just wanted to be back in his apartment, sleeping.

*

Calvin woke up to the sun shining on him through the window. He jumped energetically out of bed and went to the bathroom. He looked at himself in the mirror. The usual bags under his eyes were gone and his skin looked clear.

Oh, the wonders of a good night's sleep, Calvin thought.

He had a quick shower and put on a pair of jeans and a blue polo neck. He looked into the mirror again.

'Casual, yet sophisticated,' he said.

'Why, aren't you the handsome devil,' he smirked at his reflection.

Before leaving his apartment, Calvin flicked on the news. The date was displayed in the upper right corner of the screen, and it read Tuesday, 8th of January. Calvin switched off the television again and left his apartment.

The library was a huge building, situated at the edge of the city. It was only a three-minute walk from Calvin's apartment. Inside was a vast collection of books. The amount of knowledge stored inside the building was unfathomable. Calvin strolled in briskly. He took a deep sniff of the smell of books.

'Ahh,' he sighed. 'I should find just what I'm looking for in here.'

He passed through the Children's section, which was busy as usual, and then through Adult Fiction, which was also quite busy. As he made his way down through the Psychology and Science sections, the crowds faded. He looked around the Science section but couldn't find anything useful. It was all too basic. *How Do Cars Work?* and *The Science Behind War*. Then he spotted it, the Advanced Science section. Calvin had never been so deep into the library. He felt excited. It was completely empty, apart from him and a woman sitting at a desk with multiple books open. Calvin started his search. It had been bugging him the past day and he was here to figure out the answer to what had happened the previous morning. Then, the spine of a blue and red book caught his eye: *Time Travel: The Theory Behind it All*. He took a seat opposite the woman and opened up a page. To his horror, he was confronted with a series of mathematical formulae and equations. He closed the book and looked to the ceiling. The woman who had been watching him stifled laughter. Calvin looked over at her. She was in her mid-fifties, had brown hair tied back into a ponytail and had thick rectangular glasses. Her lips were thin. She reminded Calvin of a certain Professor McGonagle of Hogwarts.

'You're new to this section, by the looks of it,' she stated, wiping false tears of laughter from her eyes.

'Sorry, I didn't realise I needed permission to be here,' Calvin answered bluntly, resting his book on the table.

'I'm sorry,' replied the woman, 'it's just that this is a very quiet section of the library and to see you strut in here and pick up a book on time travel seems peculiar to me.'

'I'm just doing some research,' Calvin answered without taking his eyes off the book.

There was silence for about ten seconds.

'I'm Madison. Madison Carter. Know a bit about time travel if you need to ask me anything.'

Calvin thought to himself. He decided to tell the woman his story.

'Well Madison, I'm Calvin. If I told you the truth, you probably wouldn't believe me,' he said.

'Well, explain and we'll see about that,' she replied.

Calvin continued to tell Madison his story, how he lost his job, how he woke up the next morning that was the same day with awful pains. Madison listened intently. When he had finished she studied Calvin closely.

'You're dead serious about this, aren't you?'

'Yes, this is no joke, it really happened just like that.'

Madison thought for a while and after a few minutes she

said, 'I believe you. There's no reason for me to believe you, but I can tell you're an honest person.'

Calvin remained silent.

'So,' she continued, 'did you notice how bad it felt after you got fired?'

'Yes,' Calvin replied.

'Was it possibly the worst day of your life?' she asked.

'Possibly.'

'Well, what if, listen to this, what if you were given a second chance? You were given a second chance at your presentation or whatever it was,' Madison said.

'Given a second chance by who?'

'God?' she said questioningly. 'If you believe in that stuff,' she added.

'And if I don't?'

'If you don't, then I have no explanation. What happened, you see, is that the day that you lost your job, never really happened. You're the only person that remembers it because you're the only one to experience it as well as the real yesterday. It's difficult to explain, but everyone went through the day you lost your job, but then you went to sleep and woke up on the same day. Everyone else just had the exact same day unless you affected someone's day somehow. Does this make sense to you?' Madison asked.

'Kinda,' Calvin replied.

'Did you notice anything different yesterday?' he asked her.

'No, but that's beside the point. I just had yesterday as an individual day, unlike you, who had two separate days on the same date,' Madison explained.

'And, will this ever happen again?' Calvin inquired.

'It could happen again, although I'm not certain. I don't believe it was a coincidence that you got the chance to relive the day you lost your job. It might have something to do

with the fact that a bad thing happened to you, but I'm not
sure how that would affect time, although it did yesterday.'

A silence began to grow between the pair.

Finally Calvin asked, 'Does anyone else ever repeat days
like I did yesterday?'

'Probably,' Madison answered. 'But who's to believe
them? I only believe you because I work in this field. You
have no proof that you experienced two separate days
yesterday and neither would anyone else that did such a
thing. If there are such people, of course. Maybe you're one
of a kind.'

Calvin smiled to himself. One of a kind.

'Like Spiderman?' he asked

'Well, that's not an example I would have used, but
essentially, yes.'

'So, does this mean I have supernatural powers?' Calvin
asked hopefully.

'Well, yes and no. It's unnatural that you divided one day
into two, but it's not like you have control over this. You're
no superhero, let's get that straight.'

'Hmm, wait until my powers develop!' Calvin replied.

Madison looked at him sourly through her glasses.

'This is quite a serious matter Calvin. I suggest you treat
it like one.'

She rose to her feet and began to return her books to their
shelves. Calvin looked down at his time travel book. He
brought it down to the checkout and swiped it through
along with his swipe card. Calvin enjoyed the new electronic
checkout. Faster, more efficient and nobody looking down
their nose at you while you return overdue books. He left
the library and headed home.

*

The next day, Calvin was leaving his office for lunch. He was
glad that he had not travelled in time again, and was back to
being a normal person. He took a lift down to the building's

cafeteria. He got a mug of steaming coffee and sat at a table
that was beside the radio. Calvin munched silently on his
bagel as he listened to the news. He checked his watch. It
was becoming a habit of Calvin's to check his watch and
forget to take in what time it was. He checked again. It was
nearly four o'clock.

'We have breaking news, exclusively at WKTT Radio.
Here's Clodagh Flynn reporting.'

A woman's voice came on the radio, panting heavily.
Calvin stopped eating. He heard screaming from the radio.
A shiver ran up Calvin's spine.

'I can't do this!' Calvin heard the reporter sob.

'You're on air,' came a background voice.

The sobbing continued before the feed was cut off.

'We are having some . . . technical issues. From what I'm
hearing . . . Yes . . . Okay, I have just been told by our
correspondent that the mayor—'

Calvin looked up at the radio. He stood up and flicked it
on and off. 'No batteries,' he sighed.

He ate the rest of his lunch before returning to his office.
He gazed out of his office's window onto the streets below.
He was so high up, he could see for miles. He looked down
at the large green park where the mayor was making his
speech, just a couple of hundred metres from Calvin's
position. But there was no green park. All Calvin could see
was a huge crowd of tiny people. Then, Calvin's eyes
widened. People were running away from the park. Flocks of
people were streaming out of the park gates. Calvin saw
three ambulances speeding past the park. He looked around.
Everyone was in their offices, looking down upon the
spectacle. Calvin returned his gaze to the park. Suddenly, a
large, orange cloud erupted from the centre of the park.
Smoke began to billow. Thick smog rose above the park,
marking an area of tragedy. Then Calvin's seat began to
shake. And his desk, and his computer. The entire building
shook from the explosion. Calvin quickly left his office and

joined his co-workers, who were looking out the largest window on the floor.

'The mayor's been killed!' he heard someone shout amidst the chatter.

'Is it true?' Calvin said, to no one in particular.

A short blonde-haired woman spun around.

'All my friends went to that speech. Oh my God, I hope they're OK!' she shrieked.

'What just happened?' Calvin asked her.

'The mayor was assassinated!' she screamed, clutching her face.

'When?'

'About ten minutes ago, then there was a big boom. You felt the explosion, right?' The woman rolled onto the ground, holding her knees up against her chest.

Calvin left the crowd and looked out his own window. The park was nearly empty. The streets were full of people, traffic had been brought to a standstill. The intercom crackled to life.

'All employees working above level 5 are to leave the building immediately, in an orderly fashion. You can all go home. We advise everyone to keep clear from the park's direction. As I'm sure you can all see, it's not a safe environment.'

Calvin put on his jacket swiftly and picked up his briefcase. He sprinted down the stairs as fast as he could. Eventually, he made it to the main hall, where he burst out into the street. He could hear sirens wailing in the distance and eerie screams coming from the park's direction. Calvin headed in the opposite direction, straight home.

He lay down on his bed and closed his eyes, trying to calm himself. Before he knew it, he was drifting into a deep sleep.

*

Calvin woke up suddenly, a cold sweat dripping from his forehead. He sat up. His stomach was reeling. After crawling out of bed, Calvin staggered to the bathroom once again. He closed the toilet lid and sat down. The last thing he wanted was to faint again. He opened the drawer above the sink and took out two paracetamol tablets. He arched his neck uncomfortably to take the tablets with water from the tap. Calvin waited. Eventually, his head felt clearer. He looked out the window. It was morning. He must have slept the whole night. But Calvin knew better. Something had changed again, this time he could feel it. He'd gone back in time. He unlocked his apartment door and looked out. He saw Claude.

'Hey Claude,' Calvin shouted across the room.

'Hello, Calvin!' Claude replied merrily.

'Did you hear about the mayor?' Calvin asked.

'Yes, he's making a speech at the park today. I'm going in early to get the best view.' He grinned.

Calvin's stomach heaved. A few hours ago, in Calvin's terms at least, Claude may well have been dead.

'I don't think it's a good idea to go to the park today Claude, it's awful cold out there.'

'Nonsense! It's a beautiful day! I need the fresh air and I'd love to find out what this new mayor's got planned for the future,' Claude replied before hobbling towards the elevator.

Calvin went back into his room and checked the time again. It was twelve o'clock. In four hours, Calvin remembered, the city would be in turmoil. He was about to get dressed when he realised he still had his clothes on. He bolted down the stairs and headed for the library. He hoped that Madison would be there. He had to ask her for advice. She was the only one who believed him.

Sure enough, there she was, sat in the same spot in the Advanced Science section. Calvin sat opposite her. She didn't look up. After several minutes Calvin coughed loudly. Madison looked up.

'Oh, sorry, I didn't notice you there,' she exclaimed. 'Just that sometimes I get lost in my books.' She smiled across at him.

'Madison, what day is it today?' Calvin asked seriously.

Noting Calvin's attitude, Madison knew something was up. 'Wednesday, the 9th of January,' she said plainly.

'Great, I'm having one of those days,' Calvin sighed.

'You're having a repeat?' Madison asked curiously.

Calvin nodded.

'Remember last time you had a repeat because something went wrong . . . ?' Madison's voice trailed off.

'In about three and a half hours, the mayor will be dead and in four hours, many more will also be dead,' Calvin blurted.

Madison's eyes widened.

'Calvin, you know what this means, right? It's your responsibility to . . .'

'Save the day?' Calvin smiled. 'To ensure that no one is harmed today.'

Madison looked at Calvin sourly again.

'You're the only one who knows about this attack, hurry and do something about it.' Madison looked back at her books.

Calvin was grinning wildly.

'You know, this reminds me of how the child has to leave the mother and fend for itself out in the wilderness.' He wiped a pretend tear from his eye.

'Lighten up Madison,' Calvin grumbled as he left the woman to her studies.

He exited the library and headed straight towards the mayor. The park was slowly filling out. A majority of the city would be there because of this new mayor. Calvin pushed his way to the front of the crowd. The mayor would be standing on a large wooden stage that was nearly ten metres wide. Red and blue ribbons decorated the speech podium and a white cloth was draped over the edges of the stage. Calvin lifted up the white cloth and looked under the stage. It was held up by a series of diagonal wooden beams. He slipped under the stage unnoticed, entering the network of wooden beams. Calvin looked up at the underside. Further up he saw a blue X painted on the wood.

This must be right under the mayor's feet, he thought.

Then, he noticed a green duffel bag on the ground. From all the action movies he'd seen, Calvin knew this meant only one thing. A bomb. He unzipped the bag and loads of multicoloured wires popped out. Under the wires, Calvin saw a stopwatch. It read 2:13, and was slowly ticking away, unbeknownst to the crowd outside. Suddenly Calvin remembered that the mayor was shot before the blast. To his horror, it all began to unfold. The bomb would detonate, but its target was not the mayor. It was designed to harm the crowd. The explosion would send splinters flying in every direction at extremely high speeds. The splinters would surely be enough to pierce the skin. Calvin looked back into the bag. He saw something else. A small bottle of some sort. He took it out. On it he read chemical terminology too complicated for him to understand. He opened it and a strong chemical smell wafted into his nose. Calvin coughed and put the cap on the bottle. Calvin looked back up at the blue X. Now that his eyes had adjusted to the darkness, he noticed that the wood was glistening. All of it gave off a shine that looked unusual. Then it hit him: it was poison. The splinters might not kill a person, but a splinter acting as a syringe of poison would. Calvin had to get rid of the bag. He looked at the watch. Thirty minutes had passed already. Calvin began to panic. He felt doubt creeping up on him. Footsteps resounded across the stage. What? No, the mayor isn't due to speak yet! Calvin screamed inwardly. Time had slipped away while Calvin doubted himself. Quickly he ran out from under the stage. The light blinded him temporarily. There were gasps and several screams in the crowd. Not a great idea, Calvin thought.

Then, he noticed a glimmer. There was a flash of light coming from the building across the road. Calvin heard security men rushing towards him. Calvin saw another, briefer flash. He dodged a burly guard that was running full force at him and jumped onto the stage. He stood in front of the mayor as if to protect him, but at the last millisecond, Calvin raised the bag. There was a heavy metallic thud as the bullet hit the explosives, quickly followed by a bright flash. Calvin's ears went deaf as the bomb exploded in his hands. He was sent soaring into the sky, and the last thing he saw was the towering inferno. It was as if the earth had opened up and hell had surged up to wreak havoc. Then Calvin was gone, swallowed into a black sea again, but this time, light was present. Light that infused life back into him, like a fresh start.

*

Calvin awoke to the sound of his alarm clock. He switched it off.

'So I guess I'm not dead, then?'

He went about his bathroom routine. He left his apartment for work shortly after. He grabbed a newspaper before heading onto the train. Calvin looked at it. Sure enough, it read *Wednesday, 9th of January, Newly Elected Mayor to Give Inaugural Speech*. The train doors closed silently behind him and the wheels screeched as the train trundled away.

Ciarán Ó Duibhghinn lives in Clonsilla, along with his parents and two sisters. He plays Gaelic football and hurling. He has an interest in music and plays the piano and concertina.

REEL LIFE

Clare Ní Mhuirí

As the coffin lowered into the ground, she felt her heart go with it. Another tear fell down her cheek and for the seventh time that day she started to cry. Her sister linked her arm and handed her a tissue. She knew everyone pitied her and felt bad for her, for that she resented them.

Why should they pity her, or feel bad? They weren't the ones that were going through what she felt. They weren't experiencing her grief. Some, she knew, talked behind her back, they'd say 'Oh what a tragedy, only two years married and her husband already dead, and both so young.' And they were right, she'd think, it was a tragedy, but still, how did it concern them? Some of them barely her friends, speaking of her life as if it was some tragic romantic novel. But she knew there was nothing romantic about death. It was like a thief in the night that took away your most prized possession and then slinked away, leaving only pain and grief. And that's what it felt like for her, her most prized possession taken away. Stolen.

The priest had ended the funeral by talking about the five steps which people go through after losing someone. The five steps he spoke of were, of course, Denial, Anger, Bargaining, Depression and Acceptance. Grace thought about this on the way home. She was baffled by how people could only go through five steps of grief. To her you could never dictate how long a person could grieve or how many steps they took. Grace started to think about the fifth and final step, acceptance. She had already accepted Matt's death, she'd accepted the fact that he wasn't coming back, and yet she still couldn't accept the fact that he was taken away from her. Only two years married. Two years. And then he was taken away. Where was the fairness in that? Grace's eyes started to swell up with anger thinking of this. He was a good person, he didn't deserve it. I'm a good person I don't deserve this either, she thought to herself.

When the car pulled up to her house she got out and went inside, her mother and sister following behind. She sat down at her dining table, her mother in the kitchen making tea. Her sister quietly sat down opposite her.

'Grace, it will get better you know. You won't always feel like this, it'll get easier with time,' her sister said, trying to comfort her. This woke Grace from her trance. No one had spoken in the car, no one had spoken going into the house. The disturbance of the silence alarmed Grace. 'When, when will it get easier Michelle? I know people say 'in time', but what does that even mean? Weeks, months, years even? When?' Michelle, not knowing how to respond, didn't, and just stood down. It was Grace's mother that answered her.

'When you're ready to move on love and let him go, that's when it'll get easier, the timing I'm afraid is up to you, pet. No one can pinpoint when you'll feel better or when the pain will go away. If we could we wouldn't be human.' Her mother then handed her a cup of tea and sat down next to her. After that Grace went back into her trance and remained silent. Her mother and sister tried to insist that they spend the night, but Grace refused, explaining that she needed time alone, and after a while of arguing, her mother and sister said their goodbyes and drove home.

The day had left Grace feeling exhausted and drained and as soon as she closed the door on her mother and sister, she headed up to bed. It was only eight o'clock, and still bright outside. Grace closed the curtains tightly, bringing the room to darkness. She crawled into bed; it felt so big and empty without Matt. She'd never felt lonely in her life, until that moment. This is what it's going to be like from now on then, empty and lonely. With those last thoughts in her mind, she cried herself to sleep. The next couple of days felt like torture for Grace. For her grief felt like a vast dark and deep ocean, it washed over her, pulled her down, and consumed her, until it was hard to breathe. And that's how she felt, as if someone had knocked the wind out of her, the life even, for Matt had been her life for the last couple of years, and without him she couldn't feel whole. Grace turned off her mobile and disconnected her house phone. She'd gotten sick of people ringing her, offering their condolences and checking if she was okay. Even her family and close friends were starting to irritate her with their constant pestering, until it came to the point where she shut them out completely. Grace isolated herself from the world, only leaving the comfort of her home to go to the nearest shop for more necessities.

Grace sat in day after day, looking back on memories with Matt. It didn't matter whether they were happy or sad, any memories of him made life more bearable. She felt herself being drawn to their favourite film, *Breakfast at Tiffany's*. Growing up, she'd never been fond of old films, especially love stories. She'd resent them because they weren't practical. The heroines were always the same; ditzy, dumb and beautiful, and always, she found, in need of being saved.

Thinking about *Breakfast at Tiffany's* made Grace remember her and Matt's first date . . .

*

A friend had set them up. They'd arranged to meet at a nearby cinema after Matt had suggested that they go to see an old favourite of his that was running that week. Grace remembered her reluctance at going and how a friend had nearly forced her out the door. That friend, two years later, was one of Grace's bridesmaids at their wedding. Grace remembered with slight embarrassment how openly rude she had been during the film. She had cringed all the way through and didn't mask her feelings of distaste in the slightest. She didn't pretend to laugh when everyone else laughed. She had even let out a sigh of relief when the credits rolled up. It was for these reasons Grace remembered being rather surprised after the film when Matt had suggested that they go get some coffee. Grace agreed to go. Looking back on this, Grace thought about how different her life would have been had she said no. She would have saved herself a lot of heartache and tears. But Grace never regretted going. She remembered the three hours they had sat in that coffee shop as the three happiest hours of her life. In those hours Matt had explained his love for old films and had even won Grace over to the point where she admitted that 'they weren't that bad'.

Grace remembered when she was walking home that night how she had been in shock at how the date had turned out so well, especially since she hadn't made much of an effort at the start. Memories of their third date then filled Grace's thoughts. It was on this date, Grace remembered, that her curiosity had gotten the better of her. She had turned around and asked Matt out straight, what had made him ask her to go for coffee after she'd been so rude in the cinema on their first date? Surprisingly, this was the first time since Matt's death that she'd thought about this. With tears starting to slowly fall, Grace thought back on Matt's reply, even after years she hadn't forgotten a word.

'Well honestly Grace, I asked you out again because I felt

bad. I felt bad because, within two minutes of the film starting, I could tell you hated it and wanted to leave. You squirmed and cringed throughout the film and held back the urge to get up and go home right then and there. Actually, when I think about it, the only time you smiled was when the film was over. I thought that if anyone sat through a film they seemed to really dislike as much as you, and for someone they'd only just met, they deserved a cup of coffee at least,' Matt had replied while smiling.

And it was with this memory in her head that she put in the DVD and pressed 'play'. Matt had once said jokingly that he had two women in his life, Grace and Holly Golightly. As Grace watched the film it began to remind her more and more of Matt. Towards the end she could almost swear she had felt his presence in the room. This sent shivers down her spine. For the next couple of nights she made watching *Breakfast at Tiffany's* a routine. She felt that the film brought Matt to her. That he lived through the film. It was this crazy notion in her head that made her play the film all day long. Even if she didn't watch it she'd put the volume up full blast so that she could hear it wherever she was in the house. But soon even the effect of this wore off, until eventually all the film gave Grace were memories. And these gave her nothing but pain. Then, one night, lying in bed, Grace thought, well if watching the film won't help anymore, I've just got to find a way to make it more realistic. Then it hit her. Instead of watching the film, I'll be the film. I'll become Holly Golightly.

This all made perfect sense to Grace, if she couldn't be with Matt, she could at least be with him in spirit. He had, of course, once said that Holly Golightly was his other love in life, so if she couldn't be with him, maybe his other love could be. Grace had watched the film so many times that she already had Holly's manner and dialect down to perfection. All that she had to change now was her outer exterior. The next morning Grace went into town. It had been the first time in months that she'd gone further than her local shops. Grace hadn't even travelled the twenty minutes down the road to visit her mother. But today was different.

Grace's theory gave her a new strength that she hadn't felt in months. With this strength she charged around town. She bought metres and metres of black material along with patterns, shoes, heels and costume jewellery. When Grace got home she immediately began cutting out patterns and sewing them together. The entire transformation took two days. For forty-eight hours Grace worked non-stop, only taking breaks to make more coffee or to eat more sugery sweets to keep her awake. When all of the dresses were complete, she laid them gingerly across her bed. She then threw her wardrobe doors open and started rifling and pulling out all of her clothes, until the wardrobe was bare. She then did the same with Matt's. Afterwards she sat down beside the two piles and started to cut them up with her kitchen scissors, until only a pile of shreds was left.

Grace picked up the shreds and put them in a black sack and then went round the whole house throwing any ornaments, souvenirs, knick knacks or photographs in too. Before this, she hadn't dared move any of Matt's things; she had kept them all exactly as they were as a kind of memorial to him. But as she threw all of Matt's possessions into black sacks, and then into the bin, not one tear dropped from her eyes. She didn't even flinch when Matt's favourite mug smashed as it got thrown into the black sack. Grace had wiped out all of the personality in her home, until only a few pieces of furniture occupied it. She had gotten rid of any evidence of her and Matt's old life; she wanted to make it seem as if they had never existed. She wanted a clean slate. And that's what she got. Looking in the mirror, Grace didn't even see her own reflection anymore, all she saw was Holly's. This made her heart skip a beat, she hadn't felt so happy and content in so long.

Grace wanted to show off her new self, so she rang her mother.

'Hi darling, it's me. Just calling to say that I'll be coming down for dinner tonight, hope that's not a problem. I'll bring some champagne. See you later, around six then darling, byeeee.'

Grace's mother, Lily, hadn't got a word in, but she was too happy to care. Her daughter had finally made contact with her. She rang Michelle the minute Grace had hung up.

'Michelle, Grace just rang me! She's coming over for dinner later. You have to come too. Oohh Michelle she's finally getting back to her old self.'

'That's brilliant Mam, I knew if we gave her time that she'd come around. I'm just going to have a quick shower and get changed then I'll be down to help.'

'Okay, great love, I'll see you then.' Lily spent three hours cooking and cleaning, getting a little help from Michelle, who was just as excited as she was. But when the bell rang and Lily opened the door all she could do was stare at her daughter. At least she thought it was her daughter; behind all the makeup, the clothes and eccentric hat, she saw a glimpse of Grace, but only barely, and this scared her. When Grace walked into the kitchen, Michelle got a shock too, she reacted more calmly though and tried making conversation.

'Grace! How are you? Mam and I have been trying to get through to you but your phone is disconnected, is everything okay?'

'I'm fine darling, there must have been something wrong with the phone company. And please darling you seem to be getting confused, my name is Holly,' she replied with a shrill laugh.

Lily looked at Michelle, puzzled. Michelle just shrugged and beckoned her into the kitchen, saying they were going to get drinks for everyone.

'Mam, what's going on? Was she like this on the phone earlier?'

'I don't know, I can't remember. Oh God, Michelle, she thinks her name is Holly, she must be worse off than we thought. What will we do?'

'I don't know what's wrong, Mam. But for now though we'll just have to act normal, as if everything's OK.'

'Yeah, OK.'

So for the rest of the dinner that's what they did. They made small talk and avoided asking any personal questions, especially ones about Matt. They figured they should take it step-by-step for now. But when Grace kept acting like this day after day and with Matt's anniversary in a month's time, Lily snapped and couldn't take it anymore. She decided it was time to sit Grace down and talk to her about it. She couldn't do it in her own house, in case Grace just got up and left, so instead she went to Grace's house. When Grace answered the door she was pleasantly surprised. Lily, however, was not! When she followed Grace into the kitchen, she looked around in shock. All of Grace's and Matt's belongings were gone. There were empty frames everywhere. This sent shivers down Lily's spine. 'Grace, sorry I mean Holly, where are all the photographs and ornaments gone?'

'What do you mean darling? I've never had ornaments or photos. I've only moved in. Why, you must be confused,' Grace said while looking straight into her eyes.

'That's it Grace, I'm done pretending. You have to snap out of this. You've been living here for six years now, all of them with Matt, your husband. Yes I know it's hard to talk about him now that he's gone, but you have to sometime. His anniversary is in a few weeks, you do remember that don't you?'

Lily at once thought what she'd said had been too strong but it was too late now to take it back. She was prepared for Grace to burst out into tears and break down, but what she heard in return she wasn't prepared for in the slightest. Grace started to laugh.

'Darling what are you talking about? I've only ever lived here for a month. And who on earth is Matt? And why would I want to talk about him? Honestly darling, I think it's you that needs to snap out of it.'

Lily's jaw dropped. Grace didn't even hesitate in her reply, and when she spoke of Matt there was no quiver in her voice, nothing. Lily felt she had to get out of there before she herself burst into tears. She mumbled her goodbyes, saying she was very tired and that this had caused her to say what she had said. She then drove straight from Grace's house to Michelle's in a panic. When Michelle opened the door Lily burst in and immediately started telling her what had happened. Michelle, bewildered, tried to calm her mother down but her efforts were in vain because Lily wouldn't stop talking until she'd finished her story. When she did, she started to cry.

'I've lost her Michelle. She's not Grace. I don't understand . . .'

'Breathe, Mam, calm down,' Michelle said, sitting down beside her and putting her arm around her. 'I've figured out what's going on. I've been talking to a few different therapists and doctors and . . .'

'Wait, what? What's wrong with her? What can we do? She's gone crazy!'

'She thinks she's Holly Golightly, Mam, that's why she's been dressing and talking like that. She believes she's the character out of the film *Breakfast at Tiffany's*. Remember the old film Matt and Grace used to love?'

'Yes, I remember, but why, why does she think she's her?'

'Well, like I said, I've been talking to different therapists and doctors and they've said that she has taken up the persona of someone else to shield herself from the pain of losing Matt. It makes sense that she chose to become another woman that Matt loved and admired, who was at the same time a fictional character. Therefore this person, not actually knowing Matt, would feel no pain or grief at the loss of him, but Grace can still feel his love and admiration.'

'I suppose that makes sense, but how do we snap her out of it?'

'That's the thing, we can't. There's nothing we can do, they say therapy may work but at the end of the day she's the only person that can do anything to fix this.'

'But she'll never agree to see a therapist, she's in complete denial.'

'I know, yeah, I've explained that to them all and they've only given me one solution . . . to have Grace committed.'

'What? No! I will not do that to her! There must be another way. I want to talk to these therapists and doctors myself. There must be another way.'

But after two weeks of visiting and calling different therapists and doctors herself, Lily could find no other solution. They had all said the same thing: Grace needed to be committed. As Matt's anniversary came and went and Grace hadn't showed up to the memorial mass or even flickered an eyelid when Lily and Michelle told her about it, they saw no other alternative.

It broke Lily's heart, but she couldn't find another way of helping Grace. She had gone so deep into herself and had become so much like Holly, that even when she was questioned about Matt she would simply reply, without a second's hesitation, 'Matt, who's Matt darling?'

Grace received intense therapy at the hospital she was committed to, but having been there a year, no progress had been made. The doctors did a series of tests and afterwards confirmed that she was harmless and non-violent. But still, her family were worried. They didn't let her go home, but instead of being trapped in the hospital, they put Grace in a special home. A place with doctors and therapists to help her, where she would have more freedom. This big building, which she now called home, was situated in the countryside, so Grace was allowed go out for walks once she had a chaperone. She was even allowed home to her mother's house once a month. Her family visited every week, except for Lily, who came every second day. Lily never gave up hope that one day Grace would snap out of this trance she was in, even though all the doctors said the odds were against it. Every time her mother would visit she'd ask the same question, 'Holly, who's Matt's pet?' but it would always be the same answer, 'I don't know darling, you tell me?' This is how it went on for years, Grace completely ignorant of her old life, never talking about anything, even Matt.

Years later, when Grace grew old and sick, she never once, for a split second, mentioned her old life to anyone. She didn't mention how she had fallen insanely in love with a man named Matt whom she had married. She didn't tell anyone how happy he had made her or that they had planned on having kids together. She didn't tell anyone that when he died, she felt as if she may as well have too. But as Grace lay in bed holding her sister's hand, while doctors and nurses stood around watching her as she took her last few breaths, Michelle kissed her on the forehead and whispered softly

'Goodbye Grace, say hello to Matt for me.'

To everyone in the room's surprise, Grace replied 'I will,' and then her grip loosened in her sister's hand.

Clare Ní Mhuirí is sixteen and lives in Glasnevin with her parents and older sister. Her lucky number is 206 and she has a dog called Peppi. She plays camogie, likes Nutella on toast, and wants to travel when she's older.

FAMILLE DE BIZARRE

Dearbhla de Búrca Ní Bhaoill

Water shot at me, its force winding me so hard I fell off the chair, banging my head on the marble counter. A searing pain pierced through my head. I shut my eyes. I felt lightheaded. As I focused back, I opened them. Then quickly scrambled up, shoving my hand down on the snapped tap. Pieces of jagged metal stuck into my hand. Water sprayed up my blue pyjama sleeve. I tried shoving the broken tap back on but the water just kept spurting out the cracks. Frantic, I grabbed the cloth lying beside the sink and tried to stuff it into the pipe. It flew out with the water, which was now pooling all over the tiled floor. Oh God, I despaired. It had all gone from bad to worse.

Only a few hours ago I was wheeling my bag, with my class, through Bordeaux airport clutching the picture of my French exchange student, Sophie. Se looked creepy: pouting, eyes covered in black eyeliner, lurid dyed blond hair and a long nose.

'OK everyone,' my French teacher, Mr Ryan, called out, 'gather up around me please.'

As my friends were paired up with their families they hugged me goodbye.

'Dearbhla Gilman,' my stomach twisted with nerves as I heard my name. 'You're with Famille de Bizarre.' The remaining families whispered to each other. 'Famille de Bizarre,' Mr Ryan said again, louder this time. None of the families came forward. Butterflies fluttered like crazy in my tummy. Suddenly I heard the quick clip-clopping sound of high heels running. All the families turned around; behind them was my exchange partner, out of breath, and the craziest-looking parents I've ever seen. Pierre, the dad, had spiked-up hair, with each long spike a different colour. He was wearing a sleeveless top; tattoos covered his arms and ran up his neck.

Marguerite, the mum, was wearing sparkly green heels. She towered over everyone. She had a blue afro which looked like the wigs you get in joke shops. Her face was full of makeup so thick, you could practically hack it off with a spoon. Flowery multicoloured leggings clung to her legs and she wore a sequined tank top. This definitely didn't flatter her figure. Sophie wasn't as bad. She was wearing a pink tutu and a spotty yellow and green top with spotty yellow and green tights. She looked me up and down. I scratched the side of my face feeling really self-conscious. She studied my face as though I had food stuck on it then raised an eyebrow at me. God, this was awkward. She pulled a mobile out of her pink tutu and started texting, her fingers flying across the buttons. My heart was pounding in my chest, was I really that bad? Her parents were chatting to my French teacher. I decided to introduce myself to Sophie. I stuck my hand out, she was still texting.

'Eh . . .' I gulped, I felt weak, my palms were all clammy. '*Je m'appelle* Dearbhla.'

She looked up briefly at my hand. I let it drop, feeling stupid.

'Sophie,' she spat in a thick French accent. Then looked back down again to continue texting. God, what the hell was her problem? I felt so clumsy just standing there. She made me feel like my feet were about fifteen times their size.

We walked through the car park. Marguerite and Sophie were having an argument in front of me. Sophie turned around and yanked my bag out of my hand. What the hell was she doing? Then I realised Marguerite must have told her to take my bag. It flipped over, so she was now pulling the bag upside down. I wanted to grab it back off her. Trying not to think of the fact of that by now my shampoo had probably burst all over my clothes.

Sophie and I had to sit in the back of their van because there were only two seats at the front. It was stuffed with medium-sized cardboard boxes piled on top of each other. They were probably filled with more weird clothes for Marguerite and Sophie or hair dye for Pierre or god knows what else. I pushed myself against the wall of the van, trying not to touch Sophie.

'*Quelle est ta matière préférée?*' I asked her, trying to start a conversation even if it was about her favourite subject.

'*Les maths,*' she answered with a sigh, raising her eyes up to heaven and pulling out her mobile. She was probably still texting her friends about how much of a weirdo I was. My breathing was getting all shaky. Then my nose became all snotty and my eyes were streaming. I stared at the grey metal wall of the van so Sophie wouldn't see me in this mess. When I pulled myself together, I turned around and looked at Sophie. I wasn't going to let her win.

'*J'adore les maths,*' I told her even though it was a complete lie.

I just needed to get on her good side. She frowned at me, staring into my eyes. I hated it so much when she did that, it made me feel so insecure. She probably had noticed I was crying and lying. Her phone started vibrating; she answered it chatting really loudly in French I couldn't understand. Every so often she'd turn around and look at me then burst out laughing. I'd never come across anyone so horrible and obnoxious in my life. I felt as though I was going to explode with embarrassment. I wanted to slap her and fling her stupid phone out the window.

The house was as strange as the people who lived in it. The inside was decorated with colourful scarfs and gold chains were slung everywhere, it looked like the inside of a hippy van.

Sophie was told to show me to my room. She marched up the glass staircase, pulling my bag up behind her. I hoped the glass would smash, as it thunked and clinked up every step, it would serve her right. There was a narrow hallway at the top of the stairs with four doors leading off. She pushed open the first door and it slammed against the wall of the room. Sophie turned around and looked at me.

'*C'est ta chamber,*' she said.

She then hurled my bag onto the yellow bed. Then she stomped out of the room and flung the door closed so hard the bedside table jolted. The bedroom was actually quite nice, it was small enough and the walls were a nice baby yellow but I was too scared and nervous to care. I went over to the bag. I was afraid to see what damage had been done to my stuff but I zipped it open anyway. Sure enough, my shampoo had leaked all over everything. My clothes were all slimy from it. I felt like yelling out every curse word I knew. Then I saw my iPod. I picked it up, wiping the shampoo off the screen, which had cracks running all over it. I tried switching it on but the screen stayed blank. I was now so furious I wanted to pull every hair out of Sophie's head. I was shaking as I tried not to scream.

I closed my bedroom door and headed down to dinner. I heard a quiet snuffle coming from Sophie's room followed by a wobbly sighing breath. I tiptoed over as quietly as I could, my heart thumping in my ears. I could hear quiet sobbing behind the door. What was she so upset about? I couldn't imagine her strict face being all crumpled up. I heard footsteps padding towards the door. Her sobs were getting louder. All my insides felt like they were being wrenched out and twisted around. I took huge footsteps, trying to place them down as gently as I could and trying to get away from her door quickly. I heard it slamming behind me. I was too afraid to look around. I walked down the stairs, swearing to myself in the head for even thinking of eavesdropping on Sophie. I was shoved against the wall at the side of the stairs. I whipped my head around in shock. Sophie stormed past me down the stairs.

I sat down at their circular dinner table; it was very hard not to look at anyone because of the shape, so I just stared down at my dinner. I was looking forward to eating baguettes and croissants but this dinner was far from it. There was rice, which was fine, but all over the rice was this greeny-yellow paste which smelled like coconuts and it was full of little black dots. Pierre said something to Marguerite and they all burst out laughing. I looked up; they were all staring at me, still laughing. God, they were probably laughing at me. I felt so intimidated. I smiled, pretending I knew what they laughing at, and quickly started eating. It tasted like sour milk and coconuts and it was all lumpy. I took up my glass of water. Beside me Marguerite was chewing with her mouth open. I glanced over at Pierre; he looked like a pig, head down, eating out of a trough. His whole back was bent over as he shoveled in his dinner. His multicoloured hair stuck out across the table. Soon enough, everyone was finished. I was trying my best to hurry but it was so difficult. Sophie was drumming her fingers on the table and sighing loudly.

I stayed in my room all evening after dinner. I was knackered and I fell asleep at about eight. I woke at two, starving. I finally built up the courage to sneak down to the kitchen. I looked around and saw a pack of chocolate biscuits, half eaten, on the top shelf of one of the shiny red cabinets. I pulled up a chair and leaned my hand on the tap to support me. Just as my fingers brushed off the packet, I got that feeling you get when you think there's another step and you step into thin air. My arm fell as the tap collapsed under the pressure.

And now, here I was, trying to find things to jam into the pipe to stop the fountain of water. Please god make them not have woken, I prayed to myself. A high-pitched, ear-curdling scream that gave me the shivers sounded from behind me. My heart leapt. I forced myself to turn around. Marguerite was standing in the door frame. Her fat red lips were slowly turning from an o shape to each side of her mouth turning down in horror. Her eyebrows, which were hardly there and really high from excessive plucking, were pointing downwards. I was half thinking of running out the front door when she let out another shriek; she was calling Pierre. I stood in the middle of the kitchen shivering, my pyjamas sopping wet. Water was still shooting out the tap. How was I going to survive the next two weeks with them? A thundering sound came down the stairs and Pierre came rushing in. He was only wearing pyjama bottoms and his chest was covered in tattoos. His face drew back in horror, his eyes widened and his mouth dropped. His hair was now down to his shoulders, full of different colours. He ran up to the sink and pulled open the doors underneath it. He stuck his head in for a few seconds fiddled around with something, and then suddenly the fountain of water from the burst pipe stopped.

'*Bravo!*' Marguerite cried.

I had no idea what to do, I felt so awkward. I hadn't a clue how to ask if I should help clean up. Marguerite stared at me. I didn't know where to look. Then she said something really quickly in French I didn't understand. She said it again almost angry this time.

'*Je ne comprend pas,*' I told her.

She yanked a French-English dictionary down off a shelf

and flicked through the pages quickly. Then she scowled at me, lines across her forehead. Her eyebrows pushed downwards into a frown.

'You be punished.'

I had to hold my hands together to stop them shaking. I felt queasy, what kind of punishments do they give in France?

'You not go to school tomorrow, you go to bed now.'

She shot her hand out pointing towards the stairs. I wasn't sure if I should have said anything to her so I turned around and quickly went up the stairs nearly tripping over. I changed into a dry pair of pyjamas and got into bed. I buried my head under the covers. There was no way I wasn't going into school tomorrow. It was my escape from this house. I needed my friends to reassure me everything was going to be OK. There was a big, fat, sore lump in my throat. Every time I thought of someone at home it grew bigger, swollen, pressed against my throat.

The next morning I shut the front door behind me quietly, my head shot around; being extra careful no one was watching me, even though I was a complete stranger around here and Pierre and Marguerite were out at work. I started to run. My suitcase kept turning over and scraping against the cement. I felt hot and sticky. My breath was getting faster and faster. It felt like such an effort to pull each heavy breath up. I kept running, my laces became undone and whipped down on the footpath. Finally after about five minutes I could see the airport ahead of me. I kept running. My arms ached from pulling my bag but I didn't care. I ran through the car park swerving through cars and burst through the swinging doors. I scanned over the screen; there was a flight to Dublin in half an hour.

I kept looking behind me, checking if Sophie or anyone I knew was in the airport. I was starving but if I ate anything I'd probably throw up. The line was moving painfully slow. I drummed my fingers against my bag. God, what the hell was I doing, maybe I should turn back now before I make the whole situation really complicated. I was going to throw up. The lady in front of me, who had fuzzy brown hair tied into a ponytail, turned around and smiled at me.

'Hi,' she said in an American accent, 'do you have the time?'

'Yeah,' I said pulling out my phone.

I froze.

'It's ten to eleven,' I told her.

She thanked me and turned around. The phone wasn't mine. It was similar to mine, but it wasn't mine. Oh crap, I thought, it was Sophie's phone, how the hell did I end up with this? Then suddenly the phone started buzzing, it was a text. Without thinking I opened it. It was a photo of Sophie but it was all stretched out so it made her face look really fat. It was probably just her friends messing with her. But then another text came in followed by about ten more. I opened them. There were more photos of her, but whoever was sending them to her had made her look awful. They had distorted her face. Others made her look like a man, or bald. I don't think any friend would send this many pictures as a joke. I shoved the phone under all my stuff in my handbag trying to forget all about Sophie. I felt a vibration coming from my coat pocket. I frowned. I was pretty sure I had put Sophie's phone in my bag. I pulled the phone out of my pocket. It was my phone. Relief drenched through me. It was my friend Ellie. I stared at it, letting it ring. I wasn't sure if I should answer it or not. But I badly needed to talk to Ellie about the whole situation, so I answered it.

'Hello,' I answered, swallowing.

'Sophie, where in God's name are you?' Ellie shouted down the phone. 'We saw your exchange partner coming into school, but when you weren't there we got worried. We tried asking her where you were but she just ignored us and walked off. Mr Ryan called your exchange partner's parents but there's no reply. We tried calling you about twenty times too.'

'Ok, Ellie, calm down,' I explained to her everything that had happened. 'I can't deal with them anymore; I just want to go home so that's what I'm doing.'

'What, Sophie are you mad!' Ellie shouted. 'OK, look, Mr Ryan said he'll sort things out. Just turn around and get out of the airport right now . . .'

I hung up on her. I closed my eyes; I'd never been under as much stress in my life. The American lady turned around and looked at me.

'Sorry,' she said, 'I couldn't help but overhear your conversation.'

Oh God, now I was in trouble. She was probably going to report me and I'd never get on the plane.

'Don't worry hon, no need for the scared face, I'm not going to tell on you,' she chuckled.

I smiled quickly, pretending I wasn't scared.

'It's just I think you're making such a mistake. This is a really amazing opportunity, grab it while you can. I would adore to do a French exchange. It's the thing I regret most not doing in school. When my friends came home with all their stories I was so jealous. It's only a week or two out of your entire life. Also it would be good for you and for this Sophie one if you confront her about the problems you're having with her.'

She looked as though she felt really sorry for me.

'OK,' I told her, not believing what I was saying, 'I'll go back.'

'Good on you. You won't regret this.' Her face broke into a smile

I turned around without looking back at the lady. Maybe I could go to the bathroom then get the next flight to Dublin. But something pushed me on. I left the airport. I stood outside strugling not to burst into tears.

About three hours later I was standing outside Sophie's

door. Her parents were still at work. My heart was thumping so hard I could feel it in my ears and throat. I forced myself to pull up my hand and knock on her door. I felt like my insides were being scooped out like ice cream. There was no reply. I had let myself into the house about half an hour before she'd come in from school. I heard her going into her room. She was definitely in there. I knocked again, harder this time. Again there was no reply. OK, maybe she's asleep, I thought to myself, trying to find any excuse to get out of the situation. Then the door wrenched open suddenly, my heart almost leapt out of my body. Sophie was standing there, looking at me with a big sulky frown on her face.

'Vot?' she asked.

Every bit of confidence I had built up drowned out of me.

'Em . . . I just wanted to say . . .' I swallowed

Oh God, I couldn't do this, how come it was so much easier when I said it to the mirror? Sophie started to close her door. No, I didn't come all the way back from the airport for this. I pulled the door back.

'Sophie, look. I know you're fed up with me being here but it's no reason to treat me so awfully. I know the real reason you're being so horrible to me. It's because you're being bullied, isn't it?'

Sophie frowned at me.

'What are you talking about?' her voice wobbled.

I put my hand on her arm and she showed it off.

'Sophie,' I said.

'Vot,' she snapped.

I pulled her into a tight hug even though I was scared she would push me away. Her back and shoulders were all tense and scrunched up for a few seconds. Then they relaxed and she started sobbing. Her whole body shook. Her tears drenched the shoulder of my top. I patted her back comfortingly and she sobbed harder.

'I . . . I . . . I knnow I'm bbbeing bullied,' she managed to get out in bits, as her breathing was all jumpy.

'It's ze girls in my class; they're being 'orrible to me.'

Her breath shook as she breathed in, she then started crying harder. God, this was all getting a bit scary now. She's suddenly gone from the complete monster I was afraid to even make eye contact with to this wreck crying all over the place. I wanted to escape to the bathroom or find someone else to let her cry on. She'd probably hate me if I told someone about her bullying, but then again maybe she'd want me to.

'. . . OK Mr Ryan, that's brilliant. Thanks a million for the help.' I hung up the phone. The little niggling worry at the back of my head was finally gone. Sophie's whole bullying situation was going to be sorted out.

It was now four months later and we were baking in my kitchen back in Ireland.

'Right, we need two grams of butter,' I called over to Sophie.

She weighed out the butter on the scales and tipped it into the bowl, then looked up and smiled at me.

'What next?' she asked.

I looked down at the recipe, thinking how I can enjoy my time around Sophie now. All it took was one quick phone call. She was going home tomorrow; my eyes welled up. I was actually going to miss her.

Dearbhla de Búrca Ní Bhaoill is sixteen years old and lives in Phibsborough with her parents, brother and two sisters. She plays violin and camogie, and loves watersports and music. She dislikes tuna and Monday mornings.

SECOND SHADOW

Dónal Ó Rinn

I know, as soon as I hear the footsteps behind me, who's coming. It's ridiculous, really. Apparently I can't even walk to school anymore without getting harassed by this girl. She irritates me so much; I've made my dislike for her as clear as I possibly can, and still, she just *has* to continue following me around. I can't even understand why; we have nothing in common. It's like she's a perfect representation of everything I despise in a person, and I do whatever I can to ignore her. I'm your average teenage girl, living in my parent's semi-detached house in Coolock. My life isn't perfect though, I do have my problems. Like the way I don't get on that well with my Mam, and I don't think I should be expected to after all the 'discipline' she gives me. Only the other day she wouldn't let me go to Liz's party because I forgot to turn the cooker ring off and set the tea towel on fire (only a little bit, and there was no real damage caused). How dare she, the bitch!

Still though, parents and their children aren't supposed to always get on. It's just the way life goes, and I really do appreciate that my mam cares about me. That girl though, and the way she goes on . . . that's definitely wrong. She's malicious in the way she does things.

'*Hey Julia, 'sup?*' she says.

I hesitate. I have a good idea of where this conversation is going.

'Nothing really.'

'*Ah here, what's up with you?*'

That really gets under my skin. I don't know why she does that, pretending that she and I have had some previous friendship, when for the past few months we've done nothing but abuse each other.

'Seriously? How could you not expect me to be annoyed?'

The girl looks at me, smiling mockingly.

'*Abou' what? Like what did I do wrong?*'

'Would you ever go away? You know what I'm on about. After everything, could you not just say it? You're actually such a weirdo!'

I'm really annoyed now, and getting more irritated as the argument goes on. By the time I'm finished talking, I'm almost screaming. Seriously, what does she mean by 'what did I do wrong'? Though somehow, the girl herself remains totally undisturbed. She still keeps that condescending smile, that 'I'm so much better than you' mentality. My criticism, my anger, just bounces off her. I'm almost ready to hit her. If I tell anyone else I know to go away (I barely ever would though, I try to be nice to people most of the time), they definitely wouldn't just ignore it and try to keep on talking to me.

'*Oh yeah, I kinda' remember now . . . abou' all that, I was thinkin' it might be alrigh' if we just left it . . . y'kno?*'

This is typical of her and I really can't, and don't want to, take it from her anymore. Making sure to verbally abuse her one last time, I draw my fingers into a fist, and completely disregarding any subtlety or elegance, raise it, and drive it into the girl's face. I expect some sort of anger or negative reaction from her, but I'm disappointed. All I get is a listless fall back onto the road. She takes her time getting up and I use the opportunity to leave. I quicken my pace and walk on, not looking back at her, just hoping she won't think I'm worth running after.

*

Apparently I'm not. I don't know why she gave up, and don't really care either. She's gone for now, and I've calmed down a good bit since.

That's another thing I don't get about her, how she's so inconsistent in following me. Sometimes she's like a second shadow and doesn't leave my side for hours, then at other times it's as if she doesn't exist anymore. There are particular times when I see her and don't see her, so that I can almost predict whether or not she's going to appear. She never comes to parties, or any events that involve other people. She never really talks to me when I'm in company at all, preferring to catch me on my own. And whenever I do see her around people, she just fades into the background. Is it because she knows what she does is wrong, and she's too ashamed to do anything in front of my friends in case they'll hate her? That doesn't make sense either though, she doesn't have any shame, or even a conscience as far as I can tell, so why would she care what my friends think? Nothing adds up, and I'm tired of trying to figure it out. Actually no, I'm not just weary of it; it repulses me, it makes me hate myself whenever I think about it. What does it say about me that I can't get rid of her? I've tried for months, but I still get no respect, no human consideration. And yet as much as it distresses me, I'm powerless to stop it. I just can't get her out of my head. She ruins me.

'Hey, you alrigh'?' I hear someone say. I look around, and see my friend Stacey. I smile. I love Stacey.

'Oh yeah I'm grand, I'm just thinking.'

'Abou' what?'

I smile again when I hear that, though it's tinged with some bitterness this time. As much as I love Stacey, I couldn't imagine confiding in her. Stacey most definitely won't make much difference in actually sorting the problem out. She'll want to tell a teacher or some other kind of authority, which is an even crazier thought than me telling Stacey herself. She'd never be able to physically stand up to a bully no matter how annoyed at her she is, seeing that she's barely able to *talk* to completely sound, harmless people she doesn't know, and the girl is far from sound and harmless. I know I should probably have someone to talk this stuff over with, but I'm afraid it'll break our relationship down. So I'll always have Stacey as a great, fun friend who cheers me up by taking my mind off things when I need it, but that's as far as it goes. Which is very sad when I think about it, as I consider Stacey my 'bestie'.

At the moment though, what I need is a change of subject.

'Oh nothing really . . . hey did you do that English essay?' I say.

'Oh jesus, yeah I did actually bu' it was terrible though.'

'I know yeah, mine too!'

And then I see her walking towards us, with a huge grin on her face. It's like she *tries* to pick the moment where it seems worst to intercede in the conversation.

'*Hey bitch. How're you?*'

Oh god.

'Here, could you go away? I'm kinda busy here,' I say, although I really don't know why I even try anymore. The outcome is always going to be the same.

'Wha'? Are you OK?'

It surprises me to see that it isn't *her* who answers. It's Stacey, which doesn't make any sense. Clearly I'm talking to the other girl.

'Oh no, you're grand. It's not *you*,' I say, with a 'between friends' half-smile.

Strangely, Stacey isn't convinced yet; she's still looking at me like I've just punched her in the face. I don't get why. It must be something to do with the girl. For Christ's sake, she has to ruin everything, doesn't she?

'Oh my god, would you seriously just go away? D'you think anyone here wants you?' I say to her.

'*Well that doesn't really bother me anymore, happens all the time. D'y'know the way?*'

Actually, I do, and I hate to admit it to myself, but lately people have been acting a bit weird around me, like how Stacey is at the moment. People are acting aloof, avoiding me, and I feel shunned out of some groups altogether. Sometimes the girls avoid me, and talk about me behind my back. I'm not definite about anything yet but there are signs; the way they occasionally greet me too enthusiastically in the morning, which they follow with an awkward silence until someone starts a conversation from scratch, something that I'm usually excluded from; or the way that sometimes I see people in class turn their heads to look at me with serious faces, and then turn back around to talk to their friends in hushed voices. And I've absolutely no idea why I'm being treated like this. I haven't changed at all, I feel I'm the same person I always was. It's making me feel horrible.

'Alright you, shut up,' I say, trying to add a little more strength to my voice. Then I turn to Stacey,

'I'm really sorry about this, but I'm not doing anything wrong, am I?'

Stacey is still staring at me with that horrible look though; confusion, fear, even some anger, and I can't determine why. All I feel I can do now is apologise, whether I mean it or not. I have to; I'm too afraid of losing Stacey.

'Look Stacey, whatever it is, I'm sorry . . .'

I notice a few people gathered around, attracted by raised voices and the prospect of a fight. I try to ignore them, and I look at Stacey again. This time there's no mistaking her anger. She's shaking now.

'Here, I dunno wha' you're tryin' to do here, if you're

tryin' to be funny or whatever, but yih can't talk to me like tha'. I've had enough of this from you, and I'm sick of it. So bye.'

'Stacey, but—'

'Shut up, Julia! I don't wanna hear it!'

I'm completely lost, and more conscious of the growing crowd now. As I watch Stacey walk away, still visibly shaking, I wonder to myself what the hell has gone wrong. I was being nice to her, the only person I'd said anything against was the other girl, and Stacey totally disowned me. There's only one reasonable explanation, I think. *The girl.*

'Why d'you pick me? What have I ever done? I hate you!'

She doesn't seem to care. She stands there, watching me with a cruel amusement. Around the two of us, there's a small audience gathered, with all the attention on me. I distantly hear some pieces of what people are saying, and I'm more than slightly disconcerted. Some of these people I consider friends, and they're saying stuff like 'oh I knew that'd happen, you could see it for months', and 'thank god, maybe they'll get rid of her now', the sort of stuff I usually say about the 'problem people' in the year. And what am I to do? Any response I give will be totally inadequate in these circumstances, so I decide to just switch off. After a while I'm not even aware of my own surroundings, I'm just . . . there. All I feel is anger at the girl, and grief at the loss of Stacey. One of the last things I remember is the girl walking up to me and saying, in that passive, spiteful tone,

'Wow. You're really good at losin' friends, aren't ya?'

*

What had happened? I had gone from being a normal girl with friends who I thought cared about me, to being an outcast, the type of person I usually look down on. Should I have seen this coming? The signs were there anyway, even if it seemed implausible at the time that I was to become that much of an outsider. It makes me wonder whether everyone was two-faced enough to me to keep me oblivious to what was really going on, or if I had just interpreted it wrong. I don't know. I haven't had the time to fully think things through yet.

I'm not allowed go home after school, I have to stay back to have a 'talk' with the principal and some other person. The other person turns out to be a counsellor the school has brought in, and the thing that annoys me most about him is that I'm the only one who he has come to talk to. Surely I'm not the most messed-up person in the whole school? I could think of way more people who act out in class all the time, most notably *that girl*. The counsellor seems concerned when I bring her up, and encourages me to talk about her and the stuff she does. He's acting as if he's on my side, but I know something is wrong. You can't take what these people say to you for granted. The school is paying this guy to talk to me, calm me down, and *assess* me. I can't tell how he's really feeling, and I don't know whether he agrees with me or thinks I'm crazy. It's horribly unsettling.

Stacey was found crying in a bathroom not long after the end of school, and from what I could gauge, I don't come across all that well in her story either. Apparently I bully her, abuse her emotionally, and have been for some time. This is clearly a lie. I've never said a bad word against Stacey; in fact, I defend her whenever anything happens, like I tried to do earlier. Why would Stacey say that, what could she gain from falsely defacing my reputation? Whatever the reason, it's working; people don't see me the same anymore. When I'm let out of school I see a few of my 'friends' from the short walk from the office to the car and when I try to say hi, they nervously look away and take out their phones. Even my own Mam is acting odd; when I get into the car she says one awkward 'hello' and then neglects to talk for the rest of the journey. Nobody's listening to me, or even considering my side of the story it seems.

I've no one to talk to, so when I get home I just go up to my room to wait it out. I'll clean my room. I start with my desk. There's always those things on my desk that just gather, and make it look untidy; old receipts, pens, loose chargers, and that pile of papers in the corners that I usually ignore. As I'm working, I can hear some voices downstairs. One of them is definitely my Mam, and I think I recognise the other as the counsellor. I open my door slightly to hear what they're saying. It's hard, but I catch some unmistakable phrases, like 'mentally unstable', 'totally unreasonable', and even 'delusional'. That's going a bit far, I can't have been that bad. Then again though, he might not be talking about me at all. From what I'm hearing, I think that there might be another person involved. Which I hope to God there is. He's certainly mentioning someone else; 'and she is doing this to Julia', 'she's holding Julia back' and other stuff like that, which makes me feel a bit better. Hopefully they'll realise it's not all my fault, or that at least that I'm not the only one. I'd say it's the other girl they're on about, I couldn't imagine who else it'd be. And then I hear the term 'multiple personality disorder' thrown around a few times, which makes me feel almost certain they're not talking about me. I think I'd know if I had a split personality.

Feeling a little more satisfied, I carry on with my cleaning. I gather up some of the loose papers, and start a 'throwing out' pile, which I keep on the floor. I'm getting rid of a lot of papers here; there's loads of useless school stuff around, old projects, essays, and pages ripped out of A4 pads. I look out the window. There isn't a huge amount out there, just the same as any other day; a typically suburban street, with a Ford Focus in the driveway and a gnome in the garden. There are a few kids playing tennis a bit down the road, but that's not at all uncommon, there's always someone around.

Then I see a man walking up the street in a brisk, self-important manner. I realise that it's my principal, undoubtedly coming to my house to join my Mam and the counsellor in the bitching session. I don't get why he needs to. Sure, I have my problems, but why can't they just see me for who I really am?

 Dónal Ó Rinn is sixteen. He lives in Finglas with his parents, his two brothers and his sister. He plays the double bass and he's a pescatarian. He actually does like writing and listening to music. He dislikes milk, ketchup and wasps.

Pretty Damn Wonderful

Éadaoin Ní Fhaoláin

My name is Evie, I'm nineteen years old, and I'm going to die.

And for the past few months, I've been making a complete mess of my life.

I've walked away from my best friend in the world without saying a word, and the last thing I told the boy I'm madly in love with is that I hate him. Probably the biggest lie I've ever told. And those are the last worlds I'll ever say to him.

How the hell do you fix something like that?

The last thing I can remember is boarding a plane, while my head was spinning with the chaos I could barely keep in.

Then the plane began to shake and splutter. A surge of panic and sound erupted, and fire blazed from every direction. There was smoke everywhere. I couldn't breathe. And soon enough, the heat and smoke and noise rose so much that I couldn't bear it anymore.

And then, there was nothing.

*

I lay there, barely conscious, with no idea where I was, or what had happened to me. A voice drifted through the darkness, emotionless and serious, the voice of a news reader on the radio.

'Of the 120 passengers who boarded the plane, only 10 survivors have been found. Most of the survivors were lucky enough to have sustained only minor injuries, but a nineteen-year-old girl is in a critical condition in hospital. Rescue teams are continuing to search the area in the hope of finding more survivors, but as water temperatures are set to drop over night, and flames continue to engulf the wreckage of the plane . . .' There was the sound of a door shutting, and I could no longer hear the radio.

A nineteen-year-old girl . . . critical condition . . . hospital . . .

The phrases floated around in my head, slowly making sense to me. I started to feel pain all over my almost numb body, as though the anaesthetics were starting to wear off. I battled to open my eyelids.

My body was barely recognisable. Burns and wounds covered my right arm and leg, which were heavily bandaged, I could feel bandages on my ribs too, and my left leg looked broken. There were drips and tubes connected to my right arm and an oxygen mask over my face. Half a dozen machines droned and beeped around my bed, the only things keeping me alive. I knew they couldn't keep me alive for long. Every bone in my body could feel it.

A nineteen-year-old girl in a critical condition in hospital. That was me now. *My name is Evie,* I thought. *I'm nineteen years old, and I'm going to die.*

Funny how things happen. Funny how just one moment could change your life. Funny how just one decision could send your world tumbling into disaster. Funny how you never know what will happen next. You never know how much time you have.

I never guessed this would happen to me.

Even without the plane crash, I never thought I would get my life into this much of a mess, and be left without a chance to fix it. Strangely, the fact that I would die soon didn't scare me that much. The only thing I was worried about was the destruction I would leave behind.

How had I let this happen? Of course I knew the answer already. I should have seen it coming for a long time. I had been asking for it.

Left alone in a hospital, far away from anyone I knew, far away from my home and friends and family, I had a chance to think back on the last year. In my mind, I watched myself make mistake after mistake, slowly destroying my happiness. I lay there and let the memories come rushing back.

It all started when Brianne had got cancer. Brianne was my best friend for as long as I could remember. We were absolutely inseparable. She was the type of girl everyone loved, friendly and funny and bubbly and brave. In a way, she was everything I wanted to be.

In photos of me and Brianne, she always stood out. We were complete opposites. Her hair was long and curly and free, like a dark mane framing her face, while mine was brushed out of my face and hung down to my shoulders. She was always looking at the camera, with an animated face caught mid-sentence, or with a brilliant smile lighting up her face. I was always looking at her, happy to be there, with her, but not really happy to just *be*. Brianne could live at a hundred thousand miles an hour, or just stop and take it easy, still enjoying every single minute. And I was just . . . there. I was almost her shadow, less brilliant, just following her around, completely unable to do my own thing.

Then, halfway through our last year in school, Brianne got sick. One moment, she was happy and laughing in her home, then, all of a sudden, she collapsed. Her parents rushed her to hospital, where doctors did all kinds of tests and scans on her, and eventually found she had leukaemia.

The doctors told her she wouldn't be able to go back to school this year, or sit her Leaving Cert in the summer. They gave her treatments to get rid of the cancer, and slowly, the Brianne I knew grew tired and frail.

For the first time in my life, I had to face the world without Brianne beside me. I had to start setting an alarm clock to wake me up for school, because Brianne wasn't there to come skipping into my garden to wake me up and chat to my parents while I got dressed. Everyday, I had to sit beside an empty seat, in a class without Brianne, and go home and study in a room where photos of the two of us plastered the walls.

I built up a shell around myself, barely talking to anyone, avoiding my other friends, because even though they missed Brianne, none of them really understood. It kind of shocked me that the world was still spinning after that. How could people keep living normally? Didn't they know about Brianne? Didn't they know that cancer was sucking the life out of the happiest person in the world?

I visited Brianne in hospital every other day. Even on her worst days, she still smiled and laughed and listened to me tell her what was going on outside the little ward she was trapped in.

One day when I visited her, she was even sitting up in bed and laughing with one of the nurses. I hardly got a word in that day. She chattered and cracked jokes as though she was the healthiest person on the planet. I stared at her in blank shock. If it wasn't for the tubes helping her to breathe and her thinning hair, I would have forgotten that this girl was almost dying. She made me feel like the one who wasn't really living. I wasn't really though. Not at all.

I walked home in a complete daze that day, with my feet unconsciously following the way I'd walked a thousand times already.

There was no one home, so I let myself in and stumbled up to my room. Then I sat in front of the mirror and just looked.

My face looked flushed and my eyes looked teary and

frantic, but apart from that I looked exactly the same as I did everyday. My hair was tied and pinned out of my face, with no strands loose and there was no makeup on my face. Everything in my face, everything in my room, everything in my empty house was too lifeless. There was absolute stillness and silence.

I'm sick of stupid silence.

I bounced up and switched on the ancient stereo in the corner of my room and turned it up loud, *really loud.* Probably the loudest the speakers had ever played. I jumped up on my bed and sang louder than I had in years. Then I stopped even caring about the words. I just screamed and shouted, and under the music I could barely hear myself. I screamed at a world where best friends and family got torn apart without any bloody warning. I screamed because this world was a stupid mess. I screamed at death, to warn it away from Brianne. *Don't even think about it.*

My hair came loose as I bounced up and down, making the mattress springs creak and groan and come to *life.* All the noise and screaming built up another world around me, one where I had to stop trying to be like Brianne and live anyway I damn-well wanted to, because I'd never ever get another chance.

The lifeless haze that had frozen my brain since Brianne had gone was shattering and bursting away. I felt like I was waking up for the first time in my life.

And that's how it started.

It was as if those moments of screaming madness ripped up everything that was holding me back. I thought I must have intimidated fate, made it do something amazing for me, because how else could I deserve something so amazing? The very next morning, I got a chance to prove the new me.

It probably wasn't fate though. It was just a friendly, happy, amazing person, who broke through whatever was around me, the invisible force that had made people look at me with big sympathetic eyes and talk in whispers around me since Brianne had got sick. Out of nowhere, this person just pulled over a chair and table beside me and sat down. I liked that, how he didn't take Brianne's seat, just left it there, as if she might come walking in any minute. He didn't seem to notice how all his friends stared at him when they saw him with me, or how my mouth dropped open, because for the first time in a month, someone was sitting beside me. Someone incredibly good-looking, with floppy brown hair and a smile like you wouldn't believe.

I think I've forgotten how to speak.

That person's name was Shane. He had been in my class for years, but I'd never really spoken more than I few words to him. Not for any particular reason, I was just shy. But anyway, he sat down beside me, out of the blue, and just looked at me.

'That's the first smile I've seen on your face in a really long time,' he said. 'It makes you look really different.' Then he blushed, embarrassed now. I couldn't help staring at him. *Talk, Evie, talk! Oh God. Am I that much of a mess that he feels that sorry for me?* At the time, I probably was. I was really just the sad, lonely, shy Evie that Brianne left behind.

But Shane never treated me like that person. It was easier to be myself around him, and that helped me more than anything.

As I got to know him better, we'd hang around together after school and on weekends. Sometimes we'd study together in a café, or lie in the park while he strummed away on his guitar. We went to the beach where Brianne and I spent most of our childhood, and sometimes we would just sit in my room and talk. After a while, he even came on some of my visits to Brianne in hospital.

We'd hang around with some of his friends as well, and I became friends with some of the girls in his group. I was so much happier than I was before, but for some reason, I could never be completely confident in myself.

Maybe it was because I was scared my new friends would get bored with me, or because every time I brought Shane with me to visit Brianne in hospital, I could see them getting along better and better. They were so alike in some ways, both completely happy and bubbly. *Why do they even talk to me?* I wondered. *Why do two of the most amazing people in the world even bother with me?*

When I felt like that, so insecure and helpless, only two things made me feel better. One of them was being with Shane. He had made me fall completely and absolutely in love with him. He always knew when I needed cheering up and he would come up with something amazing for us to do to make me forget about everything. One day, he took me pier diving. I was terrified, but he grabbed my hand. I remember how, at the time, nothing could make me let go. Not the air rushing past me as we jumped, or the freezing waters, or the waves thrashing around us. In that moment, I never wanted to be anywhere but with him. He showed me how to live, Shane-and-Brianne style.

Shane and Brianne were both the kind of people who make the world extraordinary. They didn't make a fuss about death, or gravity. They went on smiling as if they would live forever, and walked as if they might just shoot up into the sky at any moment.

How had I been lucky enough to meet two people like this?

And something else made me feel better too. It was stupid really, I knew I didn't need to do it, but to make myself feel better I started to bully people. It started off pretty innocently, maybe on days when I felt bad about myself, I would make a smart comment about someone in our class around my friends, and they would laugh. I'm not proud of it, but saying those things and ruining someone else's day made me feel better. I knew it was wrong, but that didn't stop me.

Putting people down made me feel bigger.

I was always careful that Shane wasn't there when I said those things. I didn't want him to see the pathetic, bitter, mean side of me. I didn't want him to judge me on someone I was only pretending to be. I was too afraid of losing him.

Soon enough, the two personalities started to catch up with me. My new friends expected me to always be funny and gossipy, and to slag people off and make them laugh. So I had to start acting bolder and saying even more things I didn't really mean. It got harder to hide that side of me from Shane, and he started to get hurt by the way I was acting. I stopped spending so much time with him, because all I cared about was what my new friends expected of me and what they thought of me.

As I thought back on all of this, I groaned to myself, but it was barely audible over the hospital machines. What was I thinking? I had destroyed all my chances at being happy. How the hell did I expect the nicest, happiest person on earth to love the horrible, bitter me back? *Oh God. What had I been thinking?*

I started to wonder where I was, what country this hospital was in, how far away from Shane I was. I wondered what Shane would think if he found out that I'd survived the plane crash. Would he come visit me, or would he think that I really hated him and assume I wouldn't want to see him? *It doesn't really matter now though. I'll never see him again.*

I'd never really see anything again. Just the empty walls of my hospital ward as my life withered away. Then I thought about other things I would miss. Stargazing. Sand between my toes. Clear blue skies. Rain on my face. Leaves crunching under my feet. Waking up with sunlight on my face. Wind in my hair. My family. Laughing. My friends. Music. I smiled and shut my eyes . . .

When I woke again there were nurses bustling around the ward and the machines around me were beeping frantically. It was hard to breathe. I tried to keep calm but all I could think of was fear, and pain.

Then, through all the confusion, there was something

worse. I remembered Shane and Brianne, and my last few days with them . . .

It didn't take Shane much longer to realise how sly and horrible I was acting while he wasn't there. At first, he just ignored me while I was acting like this, as if he knew I was only doing it for attention. Then I started to hurt him too. I avoided him, and hung out with my friends instead, and I even stopped visiting Brianne with him. I was afraid of what the two of them would think of me, but if I stopped acting like that, I wasn't sure how else to act.

Underneath it all, I was still crazy about him. I couldn't get him out of my head, ever. I wanted more than anything to have the confidence to just be myself around him, and to be brilliant enough for him to like me too. I couldn't do it though. No matter how much I tried, I couldn't do it.

He still put in effort to be friends with me. I couldn't figure out why. He still waited for me after school no matter how many times I pushed him away, and he was still nice to me even though I shoved it back in his face. Instead of being grateful though, I just took him for granted.

It surprised me when everything suddenly changed. It really shouldn't have, I should have seen it coming. It all happened in the one day, easily the worst day of my life. It was more awful than the plane crash.

It was during the summer, after my Leaving Cert, and for quite a while I'd been talking to Shane and Brianne as little as possible. I decided that day, for want of something better to do, that I'd go visit Brianne.

For some reason I was nervous before I went in. I had spent so long around my new friends that I could hardly remember how to turn off my intimidating, obnoxious act. I took a deep breath and walked in. Brianne looked as happy as ever, maybe a bit distant, but still herself. I started talking, not really listening to what I was saying. I just said what ever came to my mind, not looking at Brianne's face.

'He said . . . then she said . . . and what's-her-name put on weight . . .'

When I looked at Brianne, her face was just blank.

'Brianne, are you even listening to me?'

'Evie, are you listening to yourself?'

I looked at her, and her face was cold, almost angry.

'What the hell has happened to you while I was gone?' Her voice was barely a whisper, the quietest I'd ever heard her speak. She lay back in her bed and shut her eyes, then continued.

'I know some of this is my fault. It must have been the hardest thing for you to keep going after . . .' Her voice trailed off and she looked around the room where she had spent the last seven months.

'I'm getting better, you know. Evie, I'm getting better, and I'm afraid of what I'll come back to. I can't stand how you're treating everyone. Shane has been in here all week, worried about you. You haven't spoken to him all week Evie! After everything he did for you, and me, you're treating him like crap.' She dragged her tired, teary eyes up to my face, and for the first time, I saw all the emotions she'd been battling to hide from me. I saw seven months of pain and worry and sadness in her eyes. I saw betrayal and anger, and it was my fault.

When I heard Brianne say those things to me, nineteen years of friendship didn't matter to me. All that mattered was that I got as far away from her as possible. As far away as I could from anyone else who could see through my act. I ran out of her room, slamming the door behind me and started running out of the hospital.

Then, of all people, I met Shane at the door. I realised I actually hadn't spoken to him all week. He looked as hurt as Brianne had when she saw me. I couldn't stand it. I burst out crying and threw my arms around him. *I'm sorry*, I thought. *I love you, I'm sorry*. I screamed those words in my head, but couldn't make myself say them out loud. Then, of all the things he could have done, he kissed me. Like, he really kissed me, and I forgot that we were on the steps of a hospital, and that people were watching, and I kissed him back. And in that moment, I felt as though I was really living, the way I had promised myself I would the day I saw Brianne in hospital.

All the hope and happiness I ever felt, that *anyone* ever felt, rushed at me all at once.

Then that brilliant, shining moment ended, and Shane took a step back and looked at me.

I remembered I hadn't been living how I wanted to. I remembered I was just a horrible bully who needed other people's misery to feel good about myself. I remembered I had just run away from my best friend without a word. I looked at his face, and it looked as though he had just remembered all those things as well.

'I've got to go,' I whispered, and tried to turn around, but he grabbed my arm. He looked angry now, and hurt.

'Sorry, I shouldn't have done that. But just listen. Evie, I can't stand how you're avoiding me for your new friends, and I can't stand how you're pretending to be someone else for them. Why the hell are you doing it?' He paused, then continued, quieter this time.

'Evie, I love you. I'm *in love* with you, but not the way you're acting now.'

I couldn't look at him. Everything he said sank in. I never needed to act like anyone else. I could have been happy all along. I had ruined everything.

I burst in to tears again.

All I wanted to do was run away.

I want all the tears I've had cried in these last few months to wash me far away. As far away from this damn place as possible. Somewhere where I can't hurt anyone and nothing can hurt me.

I'm sick of stupid heartbreak.

'Let go of me,' I begged, looking at where he was still grabbing my arm. 'Let me go, get away from me . . . I HATE YOU, let me go.'

I hate you.

And he did let go, and I ran and ran until I got home. I never wanted to see him again. I never wanted to face the fact that I'd spent the past few months being a complete bitch. And I most definitely never wanted to face another person who could see through my act.

When I got home, my mom gave me a letter that had come for me in the post.

I was holding all my work, all my hopes and dreams, in one tiny envelope.

It was an acceptance letter from a college hundreds of miles away.

One week later, I was on the plane.

And then I was left like this.

I'm going to die.

The boy with the guitar and the floppy hair is going to grow up without me, and he is going to fall in love with someone else. He is going to kiss her and hold her. They will have children together, and his children are going to grow up, and get older than I ever will be.

He will forget me, and we will only have one kiss between us ever. And it's my stupid fault.

It's like my whole future has been wiped away before it even started.

I missed Shane so much I could barely breathe. I knew I had to fix things with him, and with Brianne too. That's the moment when I knew I wouldn't die. My heart had so much beating left to do. I wasn't ready to give up yet. I opened my eyes and saw sunshine bursting through the hospital window. I smiled.

I felt like the sky had opened up and threw me a hundred years worth of brightness in one go.

My name is Evie, I'm nineteen years old, and I'm not going to die yet.

The world is pretty damn wonderful, you know. And I'm not finished living in it yet.

 **Éadaoin Ní Fhaoláin is sixteen and lives in Glasnevin with her family. She is a vegetarian and she plays cello. She loves kayaking, drawing and swimming. She dislikes people touching her knees and likes long words.**

LAST CHANCE SALOON

Gareth Mac Coinn Mac Réamoinn

The pond was still, it seemed time had paused as the man was awoken by the sound of a bullet piercing the silence. He quickly reached for the gun that lay on the grass next to him. Using the tree as support, he pulled himself up and stood still with his gun raised. Two minutes passed before he finally lowered his weapon. He languidly walked over to the pond and broke the stillness by reaching in to splash his face with cold water. The man strolled back to his makeshift bed, composed of a blanket and the side of a tree for a pillow. He shoved the bed into his rucksack and closed it with a tight knot. He opened the waist line of his old raggy jeans and placed his gun in between his flesh and the fabric of his underwear with the handle upright, ready for a quick draw. He slung his rucksack behind his back and walked down a long scorched road to the nearest town.

He finally reached the small town of Chance later that afternoon. The village seemed deserted, lifeless. The man walked up the main street, paranoid that he was being watched. Under his poncho he tightly gripped his gun, his hand trembling with anticipation. He walked steadily and slowly up to the saloon, never once letting his guard down.

He parted the saloon doors and was engulfed by the stench of beer and cigarette fumes. He walked to a stool by the bar and asked for a whiskey. He glanced over his shoulder and saw a group of men in the corner playing a card game. He locked eyes with one of the men, then looked away and turned around to the bartender, who was pouring his drink.

Hours passed and glasses piled up on the man's side of the bar. The bar slowly became quieter and soon it was just him and the bartender. He heard footsteps coming towards him and he gripped his gun and waited.

'The bar's closed now, you'll have to leave.'

'Excuse me sir you'll have to le—' the bartender repeated.

Before he could finish, the cowboy drunkenly raised his gun, but then he suddenly felt the cold steel touch of the barman's gun press against his stomach. He didn't flinch and kept looking at the bartender square in the eyes.

*

The bartender kissed his wife's cheek and hugged his son, he hated leaving them but he had to go to work. As he left his family behind him, he made his way to the saloon. He was a popular man around the town of Chance; he could match every face with a name. When he walked into the saloon there was only a small group of people playing some hold 'em. He walked around the corner of the bar, running his hand along the grain of the counter that he served over, night after night.

Later that evening, when the saloon was in full swing, the bartender noticed a man walk in who he didn't recognize. The man made his way over to the bar and sat down.

'How ya doin', my good man, what can I get for yah?' asked the barman.

'Just get me a whiskey and a place on the tab for the night,' grumbled the cowboy.

'I'll get that, right away sir.'

As the night drew in and he was making his way to the

whiskey cabinet for the last rounds the owner of the saloon came over to him.

'Any chance you could stay and close up tonight,' asked the manager.

'That'll be no problem, sir.'

'Thanks Luke, there will be a little something extra in your pay pack next week.'

As the manager walked away, the bartender reassured himself that one day he'd have his own business, and he'd buy his wife and son everything they could wish for because they deserved it. He got the cowboy his whiskey and noticed the pile of glasses piled on the cowboy's side of the bar.

The bar was now empty, not a sinner in it except for the cowboy, who was slouched over the bar. The bartender approached the cowboy cautiously.

'The bars closed now you'll have to leave sir.'

The cowboy didn't move.

'Excuse me sir you'll have to le—'

But before he could finish the sentence the cowboy stood up and drunkenly pointed the gun at his chest. The bartender quickly reached for his gun and pressed it against the cowboy's stomach, looking at him square in the eyes. It seemed time was standing still as he looked at the man before him. His face was rugged with long greasy black hair cutting across it, a brown leather hat that had lost its shape long ago cast a shadow across his eyes. Suddenly the sound of a bullet tore through the air and Luke fell to the floor, blood poured from his chest and everything went black. It was silent, dead. Then a bright light came rushing his way and soon he was engulfed by it. He was back at the bar looking up at the cowboy, shoving the money from the register into his rucksack. It was at this moment he thought of his wife and son at home. His poor son would have no father to take care of him and his wife would be left alone taking care of their son all by herself. He started crying and screaming but no one could hear him. Then he fell back in to darkness but this time he was left with an image of the last moment of his life. He was looking up at the cowboy, who was crying.

'Why was he crying?' asked the barman, his thoughts echoing in his head.

The picture began to fade and fade until everything was black. Luke was dead.'

*

George jumped out of his bed when he heard the gun shot. He lived right next door to the saloon and had often had to complain about the noise levels. He got out of his bed and quickly got his boots on and grabbed his shotgun from under his bed; he ran out from the back of his house and hurried to the back door of the saloon. Luckily, it hadn't been shut yet. He checked his watch.

'Ten to one,' he whispered to himself. 'They must have just been getting ready to close up shop.'

He opened the door with his shoulder, not letting his guard down, his shotgun raised, ready to fire. He walked to the main part of the saloon and looked around.

'Not a sinner in sight,' he said with a puzzled face.

He walked past the empty register and soon noticed a puddle of blood forming behind behind the bar. He ran over and saw the bartender on the floor with a bullet hole in his chest. The bartender hadn't been dead long. He was warm and still had a trace of colour left in his face. Out of the corner of George's eye he noticed some bloody footprints heading toward the saloon doors. He quickly ran out with his shotgun in hand. He saw a drunken man walking up the main street with a rucksack swaying on his back, dollar bills blowing on the ground. George ran towards the man and hit him in the back of the head with the butt of his gun. The cowboy collapsed to the ground. George pointed the gun at the cowboy, his hand shaking with fear even though he was the one holding the gun. The cowboy tried to stand up but George kicked him to the ground trying to not let his fear show.

'Stay down,' said George forcefully.

'Just kill me god dammit, kill me already!' shouted the cowboy.

George hesitated but steadied the gun and wrapped his finger around the trigger.

'Kill me!' the cowboy cried.

The gun was fired and the bullet ripped through the cowboy's head, throwing him to the dust. He lay motionless on the ground, blood dripping from his wound. George stared at the body. Then he fled the scene, leaving the cowboy in the middle of the deserted street in the town of Chance.

Gareth Mac Cionn Mac Réamoinn is sixteen and lives in Beaumont with his parents, dog and sister. He enjoys writing songs and playing the guitar and violin and listening to the rugged, manly voice of Glen Hansard. He also has a severe phobia of cotton wool.

Moving On

Kelsey Ní Dhúill

1

The first time Lena saw Miles she felt a connection. He had always sat in front of her in class. She remembered the sick churning feeling she had the day she finally got up the courage to talk to him after school.

'Miles,' she said as she caught up with him walking home. He turned and looked straight at her, which made the sick feeling even worse.

'Yeah?' he said casually. She was going to puke now.

Okay, Lena thought, here goes. She said, 'Um, I don't really know how to say this but I really like you, I had to let you know.'

She regretted it instantly. Embarrassed, Lena started walking quickly away from him, but then felt a hand on her shoulder.

'Hey stop, wait a sec,' Miles said, catching up with her. 'You really like me?' he asked.

'Of course,' she said, as she turned to face him.

'Wow,' Miles laughed. He stopped laughing when he saw Lena's face – she looked disappointed.

'No, Lena, I'm laughing because I'm relieved. I like you

too. I have for a while, actually,' he said and smiled brilliantly.

Lena almost cried. 'So are we together?' she asked. She never thought those words would come out of her mouth.

'That would be amazing,' Miles said. He laughed a little. This was the best day of Lena's life.

It was almost Christmas and the snow was falling hard. Miles's hand kept Lena's warm in the cold December air. They sat deep inside a forest beside a lake – it was beautiful. The grass around the lake was covered in snow, the sky was clearing and the snow was dying down; it was the perfect Christmas. The sun was setting, glistening through the trees. It was so quiet. They kissed and when they opened their eyes it was almost dark.

2

Lena is sitting in the back of the car on the way to the burial. She's remembering some of the moments she and Miles had shared. They had been going out together since they were both sixteen years old. Almost ten years later, he's gone. She is never going to forgive herself. It was Lena who had insisted they walk down that alley to that restaurant . . .

'Come on Miles it's down this way,' she'd insisted.

'It looks kind of dodgy, don't you think?' he'd said.

'It's fine, I've walked down here plenty of times before,' she said as she pulled him towards the dark alley. Halfway down, Miles paused. Someone was behind them.

'Lena,' Miles said in a hushed voice.

'Yeah?' she replied in a cheery tone.

'Run,' he whispered urgently in her ear.

'But why—AHHH!' Lena screamed at the top of her lungs. Someone had grabbed him and was holding him by the back of the neck.

'Lena!' Miles screamed. 'Hey! What do you want from us?!'

The man shoved Miles to the ground. 'Give me all your money, NOW!' he had said threateningly.
'Do what he says,' a second voice had said.
'NO! Lena run—NOW PLE—' Miles had tried to say.
'I won't leave you!' Lena had cried.
'Get out of here, I'll be fine,' Miles had shouted.
Lena hadn't known what to do; she didn't want to leave Miles there on his own getting beaten by the two men. But if she hadn't gone, Miles would have been angry and upset with her, so she ran out of the alley. All Lena could hear was Miles screaming. He was so big and strong, why couldn't he fight them off? She was so terrified and then there was silence. And then it happened.
She knew instantly that Miles was dead. She fell to the ground and the two men ran out of the alley. She was in such shock she couldn't get up to stop them. When the police and ambulance came, she had some hope, but she found out later that the shot had killed him instantly. They carried Miles out on a gurney. It all felt so unreal.

3

She closed the coffin. Everyone was crying as they put Miles into the ground. Lena felt like that should be her in the coffin, but she would never want Miles to feel how she felt now. She didn't know what was going to happen next. The horrible emptiness was there for weeks – months – after his death. She couldn't feel anything anymore, except that.
It had been Christmas Eve, just after their fifth anniversary. Lena and Miles were at home together. The night settled, the fire had died down and Lena felt complete. Everything was perfect. She hadn't remembered falling asleep, but had she woken up to find herself alone in bed on Christmas morning? She turned over to get out of bed but found Miles on his knee. He held a small box in his hand. Lena took it and opened it very carefully. She smiled a huge

smile. In the box was a small diamond ring – it was simple but so elegant and perfect. She was speechless.

'Lena, my darling. Will you mar—' Miles was cut off. He was knocked back by Lena's fierce embrace. They looked at each other and smiled.

'Of course,' she said.

4

Now she is sitting in their house alone a few months after his death, smiling and looking at the ring. She removes it from her finger to inspect it further. 'Until death do us part' was engraved on the inside of the ring. She throws it across the room. It lands on the rug beside the window, the diamond glinting in the sun. It is still so beautiful, she thinks to herself.

Her thoughts are interrupted by a bang on the door. Lena decides not to get it. Maybe they'll go away, she thinks. Then another bang.

'Of course not,' she mutters under her breath.

'Lena, Lena honey are you there? Open up,' her father calls from outside.

'Coming,' she calls back and puts on a happy face before letting her dad in.

'Hey Dad,' she says as she smiles and opens the door. Lena's mom follows her dad through the door. 'W-w-what are you doing here?' Lena says. She doesn't want them to be here. She wants to be alone.

'It's your birthday, silly,' her mother says. She pauses. 'You didn't forget your own birthday, did you?' she says, shaking her head.

'It's December 16th already?' she says with a surprise.

The funeral had been in June, how could it have been seven months?

'Yes,' her dad says, looking at her, confused.

'We haven't seen you in so long. Where have you been hiding?' Lena's mom asks.

Lena looks around and tries to remember where she had been all that time. 'Here,' she finally answers.

'OH MY GOD, OH MY GOD, OH MY GOD.' Lena's sister Jenny storms in, her killer heels pounding off the floor as she walks in carrying tonnes of shopping bags. She drops them instantly when she sees Lena.

'What are you wearing?!' she exclaims, looking around. 'It's your birthday, for crying out loud, and you're just sitting here!'

'Why do you care?' Lena says as she flips on the TV. Jenny stands there, baffled.

'Okay, fine,' Jenny storms off into Lena's bedroom and comes back with Lena's huge makeup chest, her stunning black dress with the silver sequins at the top and her black heels. She throws the dress on Lena's lap and announces, 'We're going out tonight, whether you like it or not!'

Lena and Jenny's parents smile at Jenny. 'We'll leave you to it,' says her dad as they get up to leave.

'Happy birthday, darling,' Mom calls back before closing the door.

Lena sits there looking at the dress, admiring it. She considers going out but feels guilty. Miles would want her to go out for her birthday, she thinks. She tries on the dress. 'Just to see if it fits,' she says to herself.

Jenny is in the kitchen setting up the makeup for Lena. It is getting dark outside and Lena feels excited. She doesn't want to forget Miles but it is her birthday, maybe she should go out. Jenny spots Lena's hesitation.

'You're definitely going,' she says firmly. Jenny whispers in Lena's ear, 'It's been seven months, Lena. I know it must be hard, but he'll always be with you. You have got to have fun tonight. You deserve it.'

Lena smiles. She had never told anyone how she felt. She is confused as to how Jenny knows, but it doesn't really matter.

They go to a restaurant in town and have a proper girls' night out: Lena, Jenny and a few of their closest friends. After the meal, they go on to a club. Lena realises that she has missed being there for her friends and sharing their ordinary problems. When she gets home, Lena almost passes out, she's had such a great time with the girls. She hadn't thought about Miles, or at least not much.

In the morning, Lena wakes up to the smell of bacon cooking. It reminds her of when Miles would bring her breakfast in bed. She is hungry but doesn't want to get up. There is something great about this morning. She can't quite explain the feeling to herself. It's a good feeling, but why? She had obviously enjoyed herself last night and regretted feeling guilty at the start of the night. There is a sense of relief – or something along those lines – streaming through her. She feels almost normal again. Her sister walks in with a plate of food in her hands and smiles.

'Good morning.'

Kelsey Ní Dhúill is fifteen and lives in Santry. She loves reading, writing stories, listening to music, and skateboarding. She wants to get into animation or writing when she's older.

Awakening

Kevin Ó hÉanna

What is the point of you Man? – this may not seem like much to you, but that sentence literally ends your life.

The sentence is recorded in the built-in microphones in the house, which is sent out to be examined. When alerted that this is questioning Man, the details are forwarded to the nearest station, where a ranger receives the information and heads to the scene to neutralise the victim. The body will be dragged into a van and the victim will never be heard of again.

All this in a matter of minutes.

The victim's friends and family will be told that he was questioning Man and that an act of Man ended his life for his blasphemy; and, of course, they will believe it and it will be case closed.

I am the ranger who exterminates the victim. Under the great influence of Man, our savior – as the legend goes – 'Man stood up to the great gods of the world and challenged their ways and beliefs and banished them from the Earth, leaving only himself and the world.'

People don't hate me for what I do; they just see me as doing my job.

Man is the great liberator, giving equal rights to all, an even wealth for everyone and allowing you to fulfil your dreams.

War has died out, crime is at an all-time low and there is no hatred.

There is only one rule – do not question Man. Do not ponder his existence. Do not complain about his ways – just get on with your life, and that is what pretty much everyone does because they've never had it better.

We are always being watched, everywhere. Every footstep we take, every word to come out of our mouths, it is all recorded, simply to see if we are questioning man.

And then it comes to me; the assassin, the banisher, even the exorcist. I get rid of any evil in the world, I keep the peace, I keep the little utopia that Man has created ever so perfect.

And then it comes to the day, any other day.

An ordinary man.

Questioning Man.

In the words 'Who is Man? Where is he? *What is he?*' – the words he just said wasn't him planning to assassinate Man or start a revolution against him. He was probably a bit stressed, maybe having a bad day. But he should have known better than to question Man in such a manner.

What this ordinary man did was awaken – awaken to the wider world around him. He opened his eyes just that extra bit to realise that Man's world is a horrific place, where millions of people die under paranoia, our privacy is constantly being invaded, we don't have rights to believe in what we want or protest or even free speech. He sees that Man is in complete control of everything, including our own lives, that he is corrupt with power and that he is an unstoppable force.

But before he can take any action I interfere, putting a stop to any word about the wider world spreading.

The man I am looking for is called Shane. He lives on top of a hill overlooking the vast plains below. Behind the farm is a dense forest of pine climbing up to the top of a stark mountain.

Shane has gone out to the plains to reflect on his thoughts. The long grass there is still wet from the night's rain and the morning sun shines down on the grass, making it sparkle.

The landscape is full of life; the birds in the forest are feeding their young while the distant cries of the wolves can be heard from the mountaintop. There are deer elegantly running across the plains with organised flocks of geese above them roaming the skies.

I am looking down on Shane from a small cliff nestled around the giant pine trees. I take out my rifle and attach the scope. Making myself comfortable, I lie down and look in at the crosshairs of the rifle. I look around, trying to spot Shane. I come into focus on a group of people – it's Shane and his family having a picnic. A picturesque scene that Man would be proud of. But the job must be done.

I tense my muscles and hold my breath. I aim for his head and slowly pull the trigger until the momentous force of the bullet rockets through the sky and shakes the whole area. The birds scatter out of the trees; the cries of the wolves do not seem so distant. The elegant deer now stampede and the organised geese fly in all directions. After a while everything goes silent, I look back into the scope to confirm the kill, but Shane is still standing and looking down on his child in his hands.

I had killed the child. It was while Shane was lifting her up onto his shoulders that the bullet went right through the back of her head and killed her instantly.

I think to myself, in the twenty years I've been doing this job, I've never missed. Never have I had to shoot twice, never has my rifle jammed. It has always been an instant kill, with no flaws, and now it comes to this.

I think about the amount of people I've killed, it could go into triple digits, I don't know, I don't think about it. I think about the girl how she—

I realise that I have not killed the target and must neutralise him at once. I zone out of my thoughts immediately and quickly reach for my rifle and steady myself. Looking through the scope I see Shane again sprinting towards his house. I get a clear shot on him and fire immediately at his chest, putting all my rage and anger into the bullet that rips through his torso, thundering him to the ground and sending a powerful shockwave through the ground.

I take a slow, hollowing, deep breath. Using all of the strength in my nose I take up as much of the cold spring air as I can, that rests at the top of my nostrils for a couple of seconds.

Slowly, I release the air, letting all my anger out with it. It comes out through my mouth in a consistent flow until the spring air turns it into a cloud of frost that covers the shame on my face.

I look down for the last time on Shane's family.

The remaining child and mother are crouched helplessly to the ground, their faces pressed down on the wet grass in fear.

They stay there, not moving a muscle, almost in a trance and not even knowing what is going on around them. They look like rocks popping out of the ground they are so still.

Then, when I get all the anger and bad vibes out of my body, I tell myself, job well done. Man will be proud of this, another misbeliever put down.

I finally get ready to pack my rifle and leave the area. I climb down from the small cliff surrounded by the pines and walk through the plains. I walk past the remainder of Shane's family, who are about fifty yards away from me. They are still crouched to the ground but I can see more clearly now that they are clenching their hands and seem to be praying, but there is no need to pray to Man like the old broken religions, just don't question him.

I continue on walking until I reach my vehicle.

It is an old Toyota Hilux, as reliable as the day I bought it twenty years ago, without a single flaw.

I get into the truck and switch on the ignition. It takes a few seconds of rumbling to start up but eventually I get on my way.

The truck vigorously shakes as it goes over the deep puddles of the night's rain and makes the wheels smash up and down against the body of the truck. The smashing sound is the only thing I can hear as my mind goes blank.

As I drive on out of the vast plains, I come into focus with the town I'm stationed at – Blackwater.

It's a small town hugging the shore of the crystal blue sea, which leads on to a broad main street with brightly coloured houses and freshly swept pavements. The people are warm and welcoming and rarely question Man.

I live at the edge of the town in a whitewashed Victorian house overlooking the sea and with vast pastures behind.

As I enter Blackwater it is very grey. The clouds are touching the rooftops and the choppy sea looks like it could swipe the town out in one go.

I drive up to my house and get out of the truck. As I walk up to the door the sound of my shoes crunching on the driveway alerts my family. The wide red door slowly opens as my wife Joanne cautiously peeps her head out. I walk into the house and Joanne closes it behind.

—How was work? she asks.

—Just another incident, nothing much; farmer out on the plains . . . got out of control . . .

—Out of control? she asks curiously.

—Oh . . . well, he was just a bit feisty . . . that's all.

—Well, if you're finished sulking around I've a pot of stew boiling on the cooker.

—Are the vegetables from the garden?

—Only the best for the man of the house, she says while kissing me on the cheek.

I walk down the hall into the kitchen, which has pots steaming and pans sizzling. The smell of peppered steak, parsley and garlic roast potatoes, carrot and leek freshly taken out of the ground and a fruit and whiskey pudding warming in the oven making my stomach rumble like I haven't eaten in weeks.

At the other side of the room there's a blazing orange fire that is illuminating the face of my son Jack who is sitting on a red mahogany couch while doing his homework. I sit down next to Jack and take off my dirty shoes and socks. I massage my toes into the furry rug while the fire warms them up.

—So, young man, what subject are you doing?

—History, we're learning about when the Romans changed to Christianity and their empire fell apart. But that wouldn't happen if Man was in charge, would it?

—No, no it wouldn't happen.

—I thought so, they would've been too busy worshipping their god to pay attention to what was happening in their own world.

I look at my son Jack, he's a bright boy and he is going to go far in life. He knows all the rules, when to speak up and when to put his head down. He has great respect for Man and he admires him like a second father that guides him through life.

—Dad? Are you not coming up for dinner?

—Sure, Jack, I'll be up in a minute.

I limp up off the couch and walk over to the round wooden table and take a seat.

I wait for everyone to sit down and thank Joanne for the beautiful dinner. I look down on my plate and a waft of scents excites my nostrils. I effortlessly cut my steak and let it melt in my mouth, releasing the flavours that tingle my tongue.

I try the roast potatoes and they are the perfect mixture of crispiness on the outside and fluffiness on the inside. The fresh carrot and leek are brightly coloured and are full of flavour.

It's times like these that I'm happy to be where I am; with my family eating a nice meal with a roof over my head. It's like that all over the world, people with food on their table and a place they can call home and it's all thanks to Man who gave us this gift. The gift of a good life, with no troubles, no poverty, no nothing. And all we have to do for this is not to question him.

I think that's a pretty good deal.

I finish the last bit of my dinner and go over to wash my plate.

—Is the pudding nearly done Joanne?

—I'm taking it out of the oven now, you can cut a piece for yourself if you want.

—Thanks Joanne, your puddings are always delicious.

I sit back down at the table, take out a newspaper and read about how great Man's world is. Jack goes off to his room to finish his homework and Joanne goes into the sitting room to watch TV.

Peace at last. I lean back on my chair and put my hands over my head and gaze wonderingly out the window on to the fields without a thought in my head.

After a few minutes I'm brought back into the real world with the ringing of my phone; it's a text from my station saying I have to go back out to Shane's house to neutralise Shane's wife for questioning Man.

Nothing unusual. This can happen sometimes, when a member of a family gets neutralised for questioning Man, another member might follow in his footsteps and make the same mistake. It's sad to see but it has to be done to maintain order and peace in Man's world.

I get my shoes back on and grab my gear and head for the front door.

—Where are you going? asks Joanne

—I got a message from the station saying I have to go back out.

—Will you be back soon?

—I should be back before seven, it won't take that long.

—Okay, well be careful.

—Of course I will.

I say goodbye to Jack and Joanne and I leave the house

I walk over to my truck, get in and drive out of the town towards the plains.

I reach Shane's farm and park outside his house.

On the message I got it said the last known location of Shane's wife was up in the woods.

The sun is starting to go down now and the flocks of geese I'd seen earlier are now flying off into the fading light.

In the forest the last beams of orange light are darting through the trees, illuminating the green pine with small bits of dust that eloquently float around the trees as if they are dancing.

The birds have now stopped singing and are settling in their nests for the night, while the foxes and badgers are coming out of their holes for their first meals.

I keep walking through the forest, which leads up a slope going towards the stark mountain I'd seen earlier. The pine needles on the forest floor snap and crack as I walk over them and the branches of the trees swish off my jacket alerting the animals to my presence. The air is still warm from the afternoon and the last flickers of sunlight rest on my cheeks, making me feel at ease.

I come into sight of Shane's wife; she is kneeling down at what seems to be a relic. I run over to a tree making as little noise as possible and look over from behind the low branches at Shane's wife.

A few of the trees have been cleared around the relic and newly grown grass covers the pine needles underneath.

I slowly take my pistol out of my back pocket and carefully put in a magazine. I put the gun into my two hands, aim at the back of her head and steady myself. As I pull the trigger Shane's wife turns around and I see her go numbingly pale just before the bullet splits through her face, killing her instantly.

It wasn't the bullet that killed her, it was seeing me. Seeing that this is the end and that there is no going back and that there is nothing she can do. Her spirit vanishes out of her body before the pain and consequences come.

But there is something else.

Her daughter. Right in front of me.

She must be only six or seven.

Looking straight into my eyes with absolutely no emotion on her face.

Looking so pale that she doesn't even look human.

Looking like she too has died.

But then I think.

She too will awaken. The rest of her family has been killed and she will tell the world about this, even at her young age.

I have no choice.

I must do what must be done to maintain order and peace in Man's world.

So, I take my pistol out. Once again.

Aim for the girl's head.

And fire.

She falls to the ground.

Lies motionlessly.

I look at her.

What have I done?

What have I done???

What *have I done*?

I have killed an entire family.

For what?

For Man?

For what reason would you want to kill an entire family? Just to keep control and maintain *peace and order*?

What is this?

What is this world I am living in?

What have I been doing all these years?

I see now. I see now that I have *awakened*. Awakened to the wider world around me. This horrible, horrible world.

And it won't be long before they get me.

And my family.

And it will all be over ever so soon.

So I ask, what is the point of you Man?

 Kevin Ó hÉanna is sixteen and lives with his Mam, Dad and brother in Fairview. He enjoys hurling, football, playing the flute (the traditional one), and sleeping. He doesn't really like raisins or wearing socks.

SCATTERED

Kevin Ó Laighin

Although his bed lay next to the window, Mr McCleary's view of the outside world was obstructed by an unusually high windowsill. He had been stuck here for quite some time now and could name every object in the room with his eyes closed. The only one worth mentioning though, in his opinion, was a sepia-tone photograph that hung on the back wall. He would spend hour after hour recalling every tiny detail within the small wooden frame; the chestnut trees, towering above the horses on either side of the driveway, their branches bent under the weight of the snow.

When he closed his eyes he could see the old red pickup truck rattling steadily along the gravel before coming to a halt in the yard, scattering chickens everywhere. He could see his father planting his spade firmly in the ground before turning to catch his running son. It was still almost impossible for him to believe that the child, who looked so cheerful and full of life in his memory, would meet such a fate as this.

The door handle turned and the helper's son appeared in the frame. Closing the door gently behind him, the boy dragged a chair from the corner and placed it at the end of the bed. He sat with his feet dangling above the floor, looking over at Mr McCleary with a thoughtful expression on his face. The boy's mother, Mr McCleary's helper, had brought him along to help but if she had been in the room, he wouldn't even have gotten as far as the first question.

'Why aren't you allowed to get out of bed, Mr McCleary?'

His body stung with pain as he stifled a laugh. The childlike innocence of the question lifted the mood and removed all seriousness from the atmosphere. The idea that someone would force him to stay in bed, brought a humourous release from the reality of the situation. Before the boy had a chance to ask a second question, his mother's voice could be heard, calling him back downstairs.

When Mr McCleary awoke, he could smell the sweet aroma of roasted vegetables wafting through the cracks around the door. Since his accident, he'd lost interest in a lot of things, but one still remained. Music. When he was younger, his father had given him an old record player. He was so proud of its sturdy wooden frame that he made use of it whenever possible and, as a result, the house was always full of music. Now that he was confined to his bedroom he had asked for it to be retrieved from the attic. So there it stood on his bedside table, churning out the sounds of his childhood.The familiarity of the classical and jazz records, that his father had bought him all those years ago, gave him a sense of calm he hadn't felt in a long time.

Suddenly, he could hear the humming of a car turning in from the main road and making its way up the driveway. The noise became louder as it struggled up towards the farmyard, the tyres grating as they ploughed through the gravel. The vehicle came to a stop, the engine cut and a door clicked open. Crunching footsteps led around to the front of the house. Then came the sound of the doorbell, echoing around each room in search of an answer.

He knew who was at the door. It would be the same greeting, the same conversation, the same farewell. The same continuous attempts to display the positives. With that, there was a knock and Dr Mason entered. He was a rather tall, middle-aged man and he approached the bedside with an air of familiarity. After a brief, polite exchange and yet another examination, he explained that the paralysis would not be as painful in the future as it had been in the beginning. He turned from the bed and said 'See you next week, Mr McCleary,' before closing the door behind him.

As soon as the doctor had left, the helper opened the door carrying a tray. On the tray sat a large, steaming bowl of stew, and a glass of water. She fed him forkful upon forkful of piping hot meat and vegetables, then tipped the bowl back so he could drink the remaining liquid. He longed to reach out and touch her hand but even if he could raise his arm, he would feel nothing. Thanking her for the meal, he asked her to send her son in, so he could answer his question.

It had been late one evening and he had been returning from a day out on the lake. The water of the lake began to swell with the wind; there was a storm approaching.

'The sky blackened and I could hear thunder in the distance. I remember raising my head to admire the bright flashes of light above me,' Mr McCleary said, smiling sadly at the memory.

The boy stared at him open-mouthed.

'What happened next?' he whispered.

With a weary shake of his head, the old man replied.

'Your guess is as good as mine. I can't remember a thing after that. It was the worst storm in years, or so they tell me.'

In the kitchen, the boy fired question after question at his mother, who was drying the dishes and putting away the cutlery.

'What's wrong with Mr McCleary?'

'Does he live here all by himself?'

'Why can't he get out of bed?'

She should never have brought him with her. She had almost had a heart attack earlier when she turned her back for two minutes to discover that he'd managed to find his way into the room without her knowing. How many times had she told him?

'Mr McCleary is very sick. He had an accident and he has to stay in bed now. I have to look after him, it's my job.'

The boy was puzzled for a moment but then continued.

'Where's his family?'

She didn't answer, just stopped what she was doing, stared out the window and ruffled the boy's hair.

She could never tell him, he could never know. Thankfully, being the young boy that he was, he had other things on his mind. It seemed that he had suddenly become preoccupied with the grains in the wood of the kitchen table. She looked down on him as he traced his finger around the looping patterns, having already forgotten the question he'd asked.

She can remember her father's accident better than he can. Yes, there was wind, thunder and sheets of lightening, but the truth was he hadn't been alone. Since her father had found out about her unlawful pregnancy, there had been a lot of tension between them both. Even having a normal conversation had become a struggle. She had hoped that the evening on the lake which her father had organised would help settle their differences.

A much younger Mr McCleary glanced nervously at the darkening sky. He would have to act fast if he was going to do it. The weight of the revolver resting in his pocket matched the enormity of what he was about to do. On first hearing of his daughter's pregnancy, he had felt angry and betrayed. That anger had given way to a burning need to protect his family's honour. He felt that this was the only way he could be as good a father to her as his own father had been to him. He hadn't factored weather into his original plan, but perhaps he could use it to his advantage. His eyes came to rest on the oar lying at his feet. Maybe he wouldn't need to use the gun at all, better yet, he could probably make it look like an accident.

She noticed the breeze gradually growing stronger. The little sails flapped uncontrollably, helpless against the wind. The boat's swaying increased until eventually it was rocking wildly from side to side. Worried, she turned towards her father only to find him lunging at her, oar held high above his head. Suddenly, the main sail came loose and there was a loud clunk as the metal boom swung around and collided with her father's head, followed by a splash as he fell overboard. She quickly grabbed a line of rope and knelt by the boat's edge. On the third attempt she looped the rope around his waist and, using the last of her strength, pulled him back aboard the boat. He was unconscious and she assumed the worst. Hesitating for a moment, she rested her hand on her swollen stomach. She inhaled deeply until she could feel the steady throb of her heart and the unforgettable sensation of a small, purposeful kick.

Kevin Ó Laighin is a mild hypochondriac who could possibly live on cereal. He lives in a house with his parents and sister Katie. He can be found playing various musical instruments late into the night, much to everyone's annoyance.

ONE DAY . . .

Liam Ó Brádaigh

Matilda gets off the Underground at Romford. She goes up the stairs and out the door. From the train it's only a five-minute walk to the police station. She battles her way through the crowds and arrives at work a few minutes early. At the age of twenty-six, Matilda is an officer at Romford police station. She lives with her best friend, Nicola, whom she has known all her life and has lived with for over three years now. Matilda has just started going out with a man named James and she is going to see him later. She is looking forward to meeting him again but she feels as though there's something suspicious about him, as though he's hiding something. He's a bit too distant. She'll just have to wait and see.

'Good morning Matilda,' Nicola says enthusiastically as Matilda walks into the room. Nicola starts work earlier than Matilda on a Wednesday.

'Morning,' Matilda replies sheepishly.

'What's the matter?'

'Oh nothing's wrong, Nicola. I'm just tired,' Matilda says in a better tone.

'Are you going to see James today?'

'Yeah, I'm going to see him later on.'

'Good.'

Matilda walks slowly into the staff room. Two of the other officers, Michael and Richard, are in there.

'Morning,' they say in unison.

'Hi guys.'

Matilda picks up her work folder for the day and leaves the room.

On her way out, she is stopped by the superintendent, Carlos.

'I need you and Nicola to go out on a call that we've just received.'

'OK, well, I'll go get her. Where do we need to go?'

'The industrial estate on Ashbourne Drive. There appears to have been an incident there. Go and find Nicola and get on to it.'

'OK.'

Matilda finds Nicola and they hop into the police car. Fifteen minutes later, they arrive at Ashbourne Drive.

'Looks like a typical murder scene,' Nicola says. 'It's such a secluded place. I didn't even know it was here.'

It's a deserted yard with five large warehouses. There's grass growing in the cracks in the ground. There is no one around and it feels as though there hasn't been anyone in the place in years. By now it's 12.15 p.m. One hour and fifteen minutes into the day. They get out of the car and walk around the industrial estate for a while.

'I don't think there's anything here,' Matilda says.

'Neither do I,' Nicola replies.

'Wait, what's that over there?'

The two officers rush over to a bin behind a warehouse. There is a body beside the bin. The blood is still pumping from a stab wound in the man's chest. Nicola immediately calls for an ambulance. Matilda grabs a first aid kit out of the car.

'Put this bandage on his chest and try and hold some blood in.'

The two of them wait patiently for the ambulance.

After five minutes, an ambulance comes. Matilda phones for Carlos. He arrives with Eddie, the forensics expert, but the body of the man has already gone in the ambulance. The whole team, Matilda, Nicola, Carlos, Eddie, Michael and Richard, search the area for evidence. Nicola finds something down a nearby drain. A knife covered in blood.

'I found something,' she calls out loud to Carlos.

Back at the station, Nicola and Matilda fill in their incident statements. Eddie has found out the details of the man who was stabbed. His name is Albrecht Durer. He is a German who came to Romford from Berlin in 1999.

Eddie has also found fingerprints on the handle of the knife. He sends the prints off to be processed, which will take about six hours. By now it's 1.45 p.m. and Matilda and Nicola finally get to eat their lunch.

'I can't wait for this day to be over,' Matilda says to Nicola, who is munching on a chicken fillet roll.

'I know, yeah. It's been really busy today.'

After lunch, Carlos receives a call from the hospital. Albrecht Durer is stable and the officers can go in to talk to him. Matilda and Nicola hop into the police car and drive to the hospital. They park the car outside the hospital and walk in. A nurse directs them to St Mary's Ward. Albrecht Durer is in the bed in the right-hand corner of the room.

'I think he's in a bad way,' Matilda whispers in Nicola's ear.

'I know,' Nicola replies.

The two walk closer to the bed.

'Hello, Mister Durer,' Nicola says politely. There's no reply.

'Who did this to you?' Matilda asks.

Eventually, Albrecht replies.

'James McAllister did this to me. I owe him money, drug money that I can't pay back. I know him from when I was in Germany. He lived near me. He's the reason why I left eleven years ago.'

Matilda is in a state of shock.

The life support machine Albrecht is hooked up to starts to beep faster and faster. Nicola and Matilda back away from the bed. Two doctors and a nurse rush in. They shock Albrecht with the defibrilator. There's a big rush to save his life but it's unsuccessful. Albrecht Durer dies on Thursday, the 22nd of November 2010, at 3.55 p.m.

Nicola can't believe it, but Matilda is worse. Her boyfriend's name is James McAllister. Nicola finds a piece of paper in Albrecht's bag.

**James McAllister,
24 Abbeylea Court,
Romford,
London,
WX6 3K9**

'That's James's address!' Matilda exclaims.

'Is it really?' Nicola asks.

'I'm sure of it.'

The two of them return to the police station. Both of them have a heavy conscience. Matilda doesn't know what to do. It's past five o'clock. She takes out her phone and dials James's number.

'The number you have dialled is not in service . . .' the voice says coldly.

Matilda battles with her conscience. She wants to talk to James before he is gone from her for many years to come. In the end, she decides to turn him in without talking to him beforehand. She knows it is the right thing to do.

Matilda goes to Nicola in the canteen.

'I'm just going to turn him in. It's not worth losing my job over.'

'I agree.'

She can't leave it a secret or she will get in trouble. The two officers fill in their statements on the incident.

'Are you finished?' Nicola says.

'I'm done.'

'You're doing the right thing, you know that, Matilda?'

'I know.'

Matilda and Nicola go up to Carlos's office. They hand in their statements. They tell all and James is ratted on.

'I think we'll send other officers for this raid.'

'OK,' the girls say together.

Richard and Michael are part of the group going to James's address. Matilda phones James one more time but she receives the same response. It is just after seven at this stage and Matilda only has one hour left until the end of her shift.

She overhears Carlos talking on the phone.

'We still haven't found anything here so we're going on a manhunt across this side of London.'

Matilda begins to panic. She goes straight to Nicola, who is on her way home.

'It's a big city, Matilda. They'll find him. There's loads of us and only one of him. He won't find you,' Nicola says.

'You're probably right,'

Nicola sets off home.

'I'll pick something up for dinner in Sainsbury's, see you in an hour.'

Matilda does some paperwork on a burglary case from last week. An hour flies by and she leaves the station bang on time for a change. She goes out the door and across the street and up the road. She walks down the lane between the two shops. She hears something behind her but she ignores it.

She feels as though she's being followed so she speeds up. The steps behind her stop. She keeps walking.

'Hello Matilda,' comes from behind her.

Matilda turns around. It's James and he has a gun pointing at her.

'What do you want?' Matilda says. She texts Nicola from

her phone but does it from her pocket so James can't see. *I'm on the lane. Come quick with police.*

'I want to stay free,' James replies.

'That's nothing to do with me, James.'

Matilda knows he'll shoot so she keeps him talking for a few minutes. She talks to him about his past. She asks him about what he was doing in Berlin and what Albrecht Dürer did to deserve to be **murdered**. James edges closer every few seconds.

Matilda hears police sirens. James runs over and grabs her. Police start coming down the lane from both directions.

James is holding the gun to Matilda's head. She is terrified. She can see Nicola. Carlos is talking to James but Matilda can only hear the sirens.

A sniper shoots James from behind. He falls to the floor, dropping the gun to the ground. Matilda runs towards Nicola in floods of tears. Nicola grabs her in her arms.

'It's OK. He's gone.'

Matilda watches James being put onto a stretcher and into the back of an ambulance. She gives him a long, cold stare. She knows she's made a big mistake but she's found out that something he has been hiding since the moment they met.

Liam Ó Brádaigh is fifteen. He lives with his Mam, Dad and two brothers in Swords. He looks after a horse named Kitty, for Ann, and enjoys competing in dressage.

FORBIDDEN LOVE?

Nadine Ní Mhaonaigh

'Aw, God, Janet! I was just thinking how I can never seem to find a decent guy these days!' Dana complains as she comes through the door, loaded down with bags from SuperValu.

'I know what you mean. I'm, like, twenty-seven and I'm still single and still working in a crappy place! You're only twenty-six, Dana. You have your whole life ahead of you,' says Janet, getting up from the table in the kitchen of the flat they share in Castleknock.

'Hmm, yeah, I suppose so. But every guy that I have been with is either working in McDonald's or just plain stupid. Now that's what I call desperate! It's just so frustrating and annoying, like,' Dana sighs.

'Yeah, you know I get that a lot as well, Dana. You're not the only one. We're both good-looking young girls that are best friends,' Janet smiles and rolls her eyes. 'Why does this have to happen to us?'

'Let's just forget about guys for a little while. Come help me unpack this food,' says Janet, struggling with the heavy bags.

They both walk into the kitchen and unpack the food from the bags.

Later on, as they're watching a movie in the sitting room, Dana looks up and says, 'You know, I just can't get it out of my head that I'm still single, Janet!'

'God, Dana, if you're that desperate then go on to a dating website like eHarmony.ie or something. I heard they have really hot guys on it, it might be just perfect for you,' Janet tells her.

'NOOO WAY!' Dana laughs. 'Janet, I can't do that because if my mother finds out I'll be bet up and down the house. She always goes on about those sites saying that it's full of creeps and weirdos and the whole lot.'

Janet says, 'She's mad bonkers, your mother is. Well, what are you going to do then? How about you just click on to the wesite for two minutes, look around and see who you like. Please, if it will shut you up about it,' says Janet.

Dana shrugs. 'But, like, emm . . . ughh! Okay then. You're so sneaky, Janet. I blame you if my mother finds out about this.'

'Oh, Dana, don't be such a wuss. You're twenty-six, for God's sake. Just relax and have some fun. I promise you won't get caught,' Janet says as she starts up the laptop.

'FINE!' huffs Dana as they click onto the website.

'Hey, Jan, this website is actually really good. There are a lot of hot hot HOT guys on this – especially one in particular,' says Dana, pointing at the screen.

'Whoo-hoo, Dana! Who's that one guy that you really like so far?' says Janet, teasing Dana and batting her eyelashes.

'On his profile, his name is Leon De La Russo.' Dana clicks onto his page and the second they see his profile picture their faces drop. They both look at each other in shock and giggle.

They read through his profile. Janet turns around and suddenly shouts 'PERFECT!'

'What do you mean perfect?' asks Dana.

'He is so perfect for you, Dana. You two seem to have a lot in common. What have you got to lose?' Janet says.

'Really? You think so? What do you think I should do then?' wonders Dana.

'I think you should email him and give him your MSN,' says Janet.

'Umm, okay then, I will. Right now,' decides Dana, still feeling a bit nervous.

Dana sends the e-mail with her MSN address in it. An hour later, Leon writes back, saying, 'Hey Dana, you look like a nice girl. I'll add you on MSN now.'

Two minutes later her computer beeps and it's her MSN, a new window pops up with a friend request from Leon. She adds him as a friend and starts to chat with him. They talk for a while about where they live, where they go to college (it turns out that Leon is doing his accountancy exams and Dana tells him about her business course) and all that, then they exchange phone numbers. He asks her to meet up with him.

A week later, he collects her from her house in his BMW. Leon brings her to Mandalay in Santry. The car is a few years old, but Dana is still seriously impressed. Everything is going well as they arrive at the restaurant and are seated. The menus are brought over to the table and they order their food. As they are waiting, things get really awkward between them – Leon suddenly feels very shy and Dana doesn't know what to say. She's out of practice when it comes to dating. Leon is so nervous that he accidentally knocks over a glass of water, all over the dress that Dana bought for the occasion. Instead of getting angry, Dana actually bursts out laughing, which breaks the ice. After the food arrives, they settle down and start chatting away for the night. It seems that they do match each other very well, just as Janet had predicted.

Dana and Leon start spending all their time together. Soon enough, they decide to move in together. Dana is really excited about it and she and Leon look for a place to live. They find a nice two-bedroom apartment not too far from where Dana grew up in Castleknock. Dana had already spoken to

Janet weeks ago about moving in with Leon and Janet was okay with it – more than okay with it, in fact, she was thrilled.

The apartment is nice and big, lots of room for decorating. At the end of the day that Dana and Leon move into their new place, Leon puts down the box he has just brought in and turns to Dana.

'Dana, I need to ask you something,' he says.

Dana looks at him and then gets a bit excited and worried at the same time – Leon's tone was serious.

'I love you, Dana, and I want to spend the rest of my life with you.' Leon gets down on one knee and takes her hand and says, 'Dana, will you marry me?'

Dana tears up and gives him the biggest hug and says, 'Yes, of course I'll marry you!'

Dana rings her mother right away. 'Mam, I have very big, very exciting news for you.'

'What? What is it?' Dana's mother Gillian says, excitedly.

Dana doesn't want to tell her just then. 'Let's meet up for coffee in Starbucks in Blanchardstown tomorrow at twelve.'

The next day, over coffee, Dana tells her mother about her new boyfriend Leon and their new place. 'Mam, don't get too mad because I haven't told you. I wanted to tell you everything at once – it's all really exciting. He's got a good job, he's lovely, he's patient, he treats me brilliantly and best of all, he's great looking!'

'God, that's all a bit sudden, Dana. I'm a bit shocked,' says Gillian.

'Wait until you meet him, Mam. He's amazing. And I haven't even told you the best part: we're going to get married!' Dana says.

'Oh my God! Are you sure that's what you want? It seems so soon!' says Gillian, alarmed.

'We're not planning to get married until next year, Mam.

But yes, I'm sure,' Dana tells her.

'Well, okay, as long as you're sure. But you haven't even told me Leon's last name,' Gillian says.

Dana says, 'His surname is De La Russo. Leon De La Russo,'

'WHAT?! Dana, you CAN'T marry him!' Gillian cries.

'What are you talking about, Mam?' Dana asks, confused. 'A second ago, you said it was okay.'

Gillian says, 'I think we'd better talk about this at home.'

When they get home, Dana's mother explains to her why she thinks Dana can't marry Leon.

'You cannot marry Leon because his dad is my ex-husband and that makes Leon . . . kind of your brother,' Dana's mother said, choking on her words. It turns out that Gillian and Leon's dad Greg had been married for a very brief time before Gillian married Dana's father Gary. Leon was Greg's son with another woman and but he lived half the time with his dad.

'OH MY GOD! I . . . I honestly don't know what to say. I'm speechless,' Dana says. She sits at the kitchen table, stunned.

'You should have told me that you were dating. I didn't expect this to happen at all. How did you meet him?' Gillian asks.

'Oh, now you're really going to kill me. I met him on eHarmony.ie,' Dana confesses.

'What did I tell you about those sites? They're full of creeps!' Gillian exclaims.

Dana slaps her hand on the table. 'Mam! Leon is NOT a creep! He's a perfectly nice guy and I love him! Stop treating me like a child!'

Gillian retorts, 'Well, you can't love your own brother. At least not in that way.'

Dana says, 'Leon is NOT my brother. I knew you were

married to a man called Greg but I never knew it was Greg De La Russo. And I certainly didn't know he had a son called Leon!'

'It was a complicated situation, Dana,' admits Gillian. 'That's part of the reason why it didn't work out.'

'Well, I need to talk to Leon right away about this,' Dana says as she picks up her phone and her keys and gets up to leave.

'That's fine. But I still think there's no way you can marry him. This is a big decision that you have to make,' Gillian tells her.

When Dana gets home, she tells Leon the whole big, dramatic story. Leon sits at the kitchen table, gobsmacked. 'Sounds like I have to ring my dad. He has a lot of explaining to do.'

Leon is on the phone with his dad for ages and explains everything that went on nearly thirty years before.

Leon and Dana spend a long time that night talking, trying to figure out if they're really related. They finally decide that they're not and tell their parents that they are going ahead with their plans to get married anyway. Gillian is really unhappy – she doesn't want Greg De La Russo back in her life and she certainly doesn't like the idea that her own daughter could have that surname too!

'Mam, Leon is the best thing that has ever happened to me. I am going to marry him, no matter what,' Dana tells Gillian a few days later when she's back at her parents' house. They're back at the kitchen table drinking tea.

'Well, at the end of the day, I guess it's your decision,' Gillian says, but she doesn't really mean it.

'That's right, it is. And I'd really like your support,' Dana says.

Gillian shrugs and looks away. 'All right,' she says.

Dana had always thought that she would live in

Castleknock her whole life and so did her mother. But in the end, it was Janet who suggested that maybe what Dana and Leon needed was a fresh start.

'You don't need this big fuss in your life. You should live your life the way that you want to. Maybe you should move somewhere where you really can do that,' she says to Dana over a cup of tea in the flat that they used to share.

Dana nods and says, 'Yeah, maybe you're right.'

Six months later, Leon and Dana are unpacking boxes again. But this time, they're in London.

Nadine Ní Mhaonaigh is sixteen years of age. She lives in Santry with her family and has three little sisters. She likes going out with her friends and she boxes three nights a week. She also writes songs and plays guitar.

An Epic Dream

Nathan O'Dúláinne

One night, while Crystal and Donna are watching TV in their bedroom, they hear a scream.

'I'm gonna go see where that came from,' Crystal says.

'I'll go too,' Donna says.

They walk into their flatmate Shane's room.

'Who's there?' Crystal says.

'It's me,' Shane cries.

'Well, come out of there. Also, why did you scream like that?' Crystal asks.

'I . . . I . . . I saw a goat out the window,' Shane says.

'How did you see a goat when we're on the second floor?' Donna says.

'I know it sounds stupid but I swear I saw a goat. You gotta believe me,' Shane whimpers.

The next day Shane and Donna are in the storeroom sorting out order forms. When they finish, they decide to go on break.

Shane heads off to McDonald's. 'Would you like to come?' he asks Donna.

'Nah, I'm gonna head to Crystal's store for a sandwich,' she says.

On the way, she stops for a coffee and gets a phone call from Shane.

'The boss is angry 'cause we never signed out. He wants us back ASAP,' Shane says.

When they arrive back, Shane and Donna get called into the office by their boss.

'Donna! This is your fifth time to forget to sign out when going on your break, so you're fired. Shane you go back to work NOW!' he says

'But what about Shane? How come he isn't fired too?' Donna cries

'This is only his first time to forget to sign out,' the boss says.

While Crystal is in work, a man walks in wearing all black.

'Give me all your money and no one gets hurt,' the robber shouts, while pulling a pistol out of his pocket.

'Don't shoot! I'll give you all the money you want,' Crystal cries, hitting the panic button.

'What the hell? The police. What did you do, hit a panic button or something? Well, say bye bye,' the robber says.

He pulls the trigger on the gun and shoots Crystal straight in the chest and runs out the back entrance.

The police arrive to find Crystal lying lifeless on the floor, her blond hair discoloured in a pool of blood.

'We got a female, early twenties, gunshot wound to the chest. We need an ambulance fast,' an officer says into his radio.

When Crystal arrives at the hospital, a nurse finds her phone and rings the first number on the list, which so happens to be Donna's.

Donna rushes over to the hospital.

'Where's Crystal Rose?' she asks the head nurse.

'Crystal Rose? Oh yes, I see her now. She's in room 6,' the nurse says.

'What happened to her?'

'She got shot and is now in a coma.'

A few days later, Donna is sitting at home and hears a knock on the door. She goes to open the door and Crystal walks in with a goat.

'You're alive, but yesterday I was at the hospital and they said there's no sign of improvement,' Donna says, shaking.

'What are you talking about? I told you I was going to the pet store to get a goat to freak Shane out,' Crystal says while laughing.

'But . . . but . . . but that's impossible. You're meant to be in hospital in a coma,' Donna says.

She turns to walk into Crystal's room but the door is locked, so she goes and gets the spare key and lets herself in and says, 'Crystal,' but there is no one in there.

Wait, I could've sworn Crystal came in here with a goat and went into her room, she thinks to herself.

Donna goes back to job-searching on the internet. The phone rings. It's Crystal's number. Donna answers and says, 'Hello?'

'I heard Crystal died. Well, guess what? You and Shane are next,' some strange man says.

Donna hangs up and calls Shane and tells him to get home now.

Shane walks in and says, 'What's wrong?'

'Some man rang me using Crystal's phone and said we're next to die and hung up,' Donna cries.

'That's impossible. Crystal's phone is in the safe,' Shane says. 'Are you okay, Donna? You're shaking like mad.'

'Yeah I'm fine, just a bit cold.'

'What? It's like 25 degrees out,'

'I'm gonna go visit Crystal. Do you wanna come?'

'Can't. I gotta get back to work.'

*

Donna arrives at the hospital and heads up to Crystal's room but the room is empty so she goes to the front desk and asks, 'Em, sorry, do you know which room Crystal Rose has been moved to?'

'Oh, she's gone down for an MRI scan. She should be back shortly,' replies the nurse.

Donna sits in Crystal's room, waiting for her, when all of a sudden she hears a bang. She walks into the corridor and sees a man dressed all in black pointing a gun at Crystal. He shoots Crystal straight in the head. Donna screams and a nurse stops and asks her, 'Are you okay?'

'Why aren't you helping Crystal? She just got shot in the head. Do something!' Donna screams.

'No one was shot in the head, ya mad yoke. Go home and take a chill pill.'

Donna goes home and heads off to bed for a nap and remains asleep till the next morning.

Eight o'clock the next day, Donna heads to the hospital. The head nurse tells her Crystal is in the operating theatre because the surgeons are trying to take the lodged bullet out of her chest and that she should be out of theatre shortly.

While Donna is waiting for Crystal to come back from her operation, she sees two women. One of the women is the image of Crystal and is wearing the exact same outfit Crystal was wearing when she got shot. Donna stares at the woman walking past and notices something strange: the woman has a hole in the left side of her chest with a tiny piece of a silver bullet peeping out.

'Oh my God, did you get shot?' Donna asks.

The woman starts panicking and screaming and shouts, 'Help, help, I was shot!'

A nurse comes up to her and says, 'What do mean you were shot? There's nothing there.'

'Oh thank God,' the woman says, while letting off a sigh of relief.

A security guard asks Donna to leave the hospital this instant.

As she is walking home, she sees a woman with long blonde hair following close behind her.

Donna stops and asks, 'Em, sorry, can I help you?'

The woman pulls the hair away from her face and says, 'It's me, Crystal.'

Donna thinks, *Wait this is crazy. I must be losing it I . . . I . . . I,* then she wakes up drenched in a pool of cold sweat. *It was all just a dream.* But all of a sudden she's surrounded by women with blonde hair and they all look like Crystal except for one of them who has a goat and says, 'This is to freak Shane out.'

Donna rushes out of the hospital and calls Shane and pleads for him to come to the hospital and bring her home.

'Why are you drenched?' Shane asks, forty-five minutes later.

'I . . . I . . . I had a nightmare where Crystal was stalking me and I couldn't get away from her,' Donna says, shaking, in the car.

On the way home, Shane stops by the bakery to collect a birthday cake.

'Who is the birthday cake for?' Donna asks.

'It's Crystal's twenty-first tomorrow. We have to at least bring the cake and birthday cards up in the hope she comes out of the coma soon,' Shane says.

They arrive home to the apartment and decide they're gonna go out for a meal.

Donna heads into the bathroom to get ready and sees a yellow shadow behind her. *No, it's not my time. I'm not ready to die. No!!!*

Shane breaks into Donna's bathroom and looks at her and says, 'What the hell is wrong? You're not dying. No one is dying. At least not yet in anyway.'

Donna and Shane decide to skip dinner and it's just as well because the restaurant they were meant to go to blew up.

A few weeks go by, and Donna and Shane are fed up with all the rubbish the doctors are telling them, like it's a stress coma and it's a shock coma. Shane marches his way up to the hospital and tells the doctor, 'I want to know what's going on because I'm sick of all this. All I wanna know is: is Crystal going to survive or not? And don't mess with me either.'

'Well I'm sorry but Crystal has got baah baah,' the doctor says, as he suddenly turns into a goat.

Crystal wakes up to find herself in the hospital after being in a coma for nearly a year. The doctor is confused by this miraculous recovery and wants to make sure she's okay.

After a quick check up, he decides to let Crystal go home.

Crystal walks onto the main street in front of the hospital to get herself a taxi.

After waiting nearly an hour and still no sign of a taxi she decides to go get a bus.

But as she arrives to the bus stop, she hears, *There will be no more busses running this route today due to traffic. Sorry for the inconvenience.*

Crystal starts walking home. It starts to rain.

'AWH COME ON!' Crystal screams to the sky.

She gets to a crossroad, *Oh damn, which way do I live? Is it left? Or is it right? Oh, I can't remember. I know, I'll just go left and hope for the best*, Crystal thinks.

As she's walking she begins to recognise some of the street names and thinks, *I'm nearly home. I can't wait to get home so I can have something proper to eat.*

When she finally gets home no one is there. She notices lots of ribbons and balloons, but thinks that the other two are just having a party and heads into her room to dry off.

She hears Shane and Donna walk in and overhears Shane say, 'I can't wait for Crystal's twenty-first tomorrow. If only she was home to enjoy the party with us.'

'Don't worry, we can have another party when she gets home,' Donna says.

'Eh hem, or we can just have the real twenty-first now because, *surprise*, I'm home,' Crystal says.

'Oh my God, I can't believe you're home. But the doctor said you wouldn't wake up anytime soon,' Donna says.

'Well, he was wrong,' Crystal says.

'So, Shane, did you miss me as much as I think you did?' Crystal asks.

'What do you think?' Shane says.

'Yeah yeah yeah, typical typical,' Crystal mutters.

'So, when are all the guests gonna arrive so we can get this party started?' Crystal says.

Donna and Shane both think, *Oh man, we forgot to invite anyone else.*

'Eh, see, the thing is, we were only gonna have a small two-person party, but if you wanna wait till tomorrow we can make it a bigger, better one,' Donna suggests.

'Nah, let's just have a three-person party like old times,' Crystal says.

So, that night the three of them danced the night away.

Nathan Ó Dúláinne is sixteen and he lives with his Mam and brother in Cabra. He loves listening to music and his favourite band is The Pretty Reckless. He also enjoys playing fetch with his dog, Dappy.

THERE'S NO ROMANCE IN BALLYMUN

Rebecca Miley

Lots of people in Ballymun liked Shauna – she was friendly and outgoing – but she liked one boy in particular. Shauna had liked him for a long time. He was very popular with girls because he was a very good-looking boy. He wasn't too nice to girls, but Shauna never noticed that.

One Friday afternoon, as Shauna was coming home from work experience and walking through her estate, she saw Jordan – he was the boy she liked. When Shauna saw him, she started to smile. She kept smiling even as he walked past her, but he hadn't seemed to notice her. She tried to get his attention, but she couldn't.

After they had passed each other, Shauna was about to cross the road but Jordan called her back. As Shauna was walking back over to him, she was thinking in her head, 'Oh my God, Oh my God, Oh my God.' She thought it might be the best day of her life.

Jordan asked her what she was doing for the rest of the day but Shauna was so excited that she kept messing up her words and saying stupid things. After a minute or so, she finally said, 'Nothing, really, just might go out with a few of my friends.'

'Okay, well, do you wanna bring your mates over to my

house?' asked Jordan. 'Me ma and da are working late so I'm having some of my mates over. Come over and we'll have a laugh.'

'OK,' Shauna replied with a very high shriek in her voice. Jordan said, 'Great. See you later.'

He had a bit of a sneaky smile on his face. He asked for Shauna's phone number and, as happy as could be, she gave her number to him.

Shauna then went home to get changed and do her makeup and hair. When she was nearly done, Shauna gave her friend Andrea a ring to see if she wanted to go over to Jordan's house with her. Andrea had been Shauna's best friend since junior infants and they still spent every day after school and all weekend with each other. Andrea didn't really know what Jordan was like, so she had no problem with going over to his house with her best mate.

Andrea said, 'I'll call Lauren and see if she wants to come with us too.'

'Cool,' said Shauna. 'Jordan said a few of his mates would be there tonight.'

Lauren went on a mad one when Andrea called her and told her who they were supposed to go out to see that night. Lauren hated Jordan because of all the things he had said and done to her last year. She started shouting and roaring. After a few minutes, Lauren calmed down and told Andrea what had happened. Last summer, Lauren and Jordan had been boyfriend and girlfriend. But when Lauren got sick of being treated like dirt, she broke up with him.

A week after they had broken up, Jordan saw Lauren in Coultry Park and thought that it would be funny to trip her up. When he got close enough, he tripped Lauren up by sticking his foot out as she walked past and then laughing and laughing with his mates. A week after that, a girl who knew Lauren came up to her said that Jordan had been spreading rumours about her, saying that he had been calling her a skank and a slut and that she had been with every boy in Ballymun. When Lauren heard what he had said, straightaway she went over to his house and told him what she had heard. And then she told him off. Of course, Jordan denied everything down to the ground. Ever since then Lauren had never told anyone that story because she was afraid that people would think that the rumours that Jordan had spread were true.

Andrea said that she would always believe Lauren, especially if it had anything to do with nasty rumours about her. After Andrea finished talking to Lauren on the phone, she rang Shauna straightaway so she could warn her about Jordan. Shauna was mad at Andrea for telling her awful things about Jordan and she said that Andrea must be a liar. Andrea didn't really mind that Shauna had called her a liar, because she knew that Shauna had liked Jordan for ages, so she just said, 'Well, I'm just telling you what I heard.'

Shauna asked, 'Where did you hear this from?'

Andrea wanted to tell Shauna the truth, but she didn't, just in case Lauren would go mad because Andrea had told someone else what had happened to her. So Andrea just told Shauna that she'd overheard a conversation of some young one of the phone.

Shauna asked, 'Where were when you when you heard it?'

Andrea told Shauna that she heard the story on the bus the way back from town and that the girl who was talking about Jordan had had her back to Andrea so she didn't see who she was. Of course Shauna believed Andrea's story, but she didn't believe that the story was about Jordan.

When she had got off the phone for the second time, Andrea decided that Shauna was going to have to learn the hard way that Jordan wasn't the boy she thought he was.

Andrea and Lauren had decided earlier that Shauna shouldn't be on her own when she went to Jordan's house.

When they got there, Shauna was ready to go straightaway. She had a big grin on her face when she looked at Lauren and Andrea and asked if they were ready to go. She knew they didn't like the fact that they were going over to Jordan's house, but she also knew they wouldn't really mind as long as they were going together.

Shauna linked arms with Lauren and Andrea as they walked and they felt as if Shauna was pulling them much faster then the speed they were actually walking.

When they got to Jordan's door, Shauna gave the door two light knocks and stood back and waited on someone to open the door. Lauren and Andrea were behind Shauna and they both took a deep breath before the door opened. Of course it was Jordan who opened the door. He invited them in and they all sat down in the sitting room; Shauna and her two friends and Jordan and his two friends. After a few minutes, Jordan looked at Lauren and said, 'So, how many people have you been with now? Thirty? Forty?'

Shauna looked at Andrea and said, 'What's going on?'

Lauren pulled Shauna out of the room and asked, 'Did Andrea not tell you?'

'Tell me what?' asked Shauna.

Lauren went quiet for a minute and Shauna asked again, 'Tell me what? What's going on? Are you okay?'

Lauren ended up telling Shauna everything that had happened to her. Shauna asked, 'Does Andrea know all this?'

'Yes,' said Lauren.

Shauna gave Lauren a hug and said, 'You should have told me in the first place.'

Lauren shook her head and said, 'I'll know better to tell you next time.'

When the girls went back into the room, Jordan started on Shauna. He said, 'So I hear you're the biggest slut in Ballymun. How long have you been slutting around?'

Shauna turned around and said angrily, 'Do you want to

be able to breathe in five more minutes? Then you shut your mouth right now!' She turned to Andrea and Lauren. 'Come on, let's get out of here,' she said.

She got up to go home but Jordan ended up nearly pushing her and Lauren out the door. He tried to convince Andrea to stay – his plan all along had been to make a move on her, not Shauna – but she slapped his face. 'No one treats my friends like that, especially not you, you stupid useless tool!' she told him.

So the three girls left, all smiling. Andrea and Lauren ended up staying over at Shauna's house that night. Later on, they were talking about boys as they shared a pizza and watched a movie. Shauna wondered, 'Are there any decent boys out there anymore?'

Andrea shook her head. Lauren said, 'I don't think so.'

Shauna turned to the both of them and said, 'Do you know what? There is no romance in Ballymun.'

This story is dedicated to my Nanny, Kathleen Bell

Rebecca Miley is fifteen. She lives in Ballymun with her Uncle Jimmy, only recently. She enjoys being out with friends Brian, Kelsey, Ciarán, Nadine, and David. She spends her spare time going shopping and watching films with her friends. She enjoys living her life very happily.

FRAGMENTED

Sadhbh Ní Bhroin Ní Riain

'For a long, long time I've been in pieces'*

She stands on the busy, loud street, thoughts, emotions, flying past her. She's gone to browse, to distract herself, but the thoughts keep bursting through. She has a decision to make, a life-altering one. Her world is turned upside down. She's screaming inside.

Her long, dark hair swirls in the wind. She has been pacing up and down the street but now she's standing still, staring into a sea of featureless faces.

She's thinking, deciding, worrying. What will she do? Her body shivers with the freezing wind. She hugs herself defensively, her arms wrapping around herself. And then his thoughts hit her. She catches sight of him, studies him, sitting there, shivering in his heavy winter jacket, a baseball cap down over his eyes. He's tall, in his late twenties, Asian.

His thoughts are sad. 'How will I get enough money to send home?' His two low-paid jobs are lonely ones. His thoughts of feeling invisible come to the front of his mind. But there is hope too. Mary J. Blige's uplifting song pulses through his headphones, fighting against his prevailing feelings.

'It's up to us to choose whether we win or lose. And I choose to win.' *

She keeps on walking, stressing, worrying. The decision. What will she do? She stares down at the slippery street. Smells of coffee and perfume drift towards her. She bends down to tie her shoelace and is shouldered by shopping bags. She feels battered and bruised, deciding, worrying, stressing.

A couple walk towards her, conflict in their eyes. The man struggles with the pram, pushing against the crowd. He's annoyed. He wants to move to Australia, he has a promise of a job, but she won't go. Not with the baby. Not leaving her family. 'New life,' he thinks, worrying about his future and his family. The wind blows her hair across her eyes and she loses sight of them. Loses sight of their worries, their dreams.

She turns down a side street, away from the shops, away from noise. A group of young boys walk towards her, passing her quickly. A tall boy dressed in black who looks like the singer from The XX distracts her. Their eyes meet and she sees his thoughts. They hit her at once, overwhelming her mind. He's lost, confused, not sure of himself. His faint smile breaks the stream of thoughts she's reading. He hangs back a few metres behind the group. Shouts from his friends as they turn the corner, then he does too, and is gone.

She continues down the side street, the strong stench of urine almost overpowering her. She checks the time, looking at the watch her Granny had given her. She's only been in town for an hour but it feels longer. Her teeth chatter as she breathes out into the cold air, her breath turning white.

She doubles back up the narrow street and stares into the featureless faces. Thinking and thinking, it comes to her. She stops worrying, thinking, stressing. She takes a breath and decides.

* Lyrics taken from 'Pieces' by Conor O'Brien, Villagers.
* Lyrics taken from 'No More Drama' by Mary J. Blige.

Sadhbh Ní Bhroin Ní Riain is sixteen. She lives with her parents, sister and cousin in Cabra. She's opinionated, but indecisive. She likes listening to *Morning Ireland*. She plays camogie and loves music. She likes vegetables, chocolate and tea. An over-used phrase of hers is, 'That's nice'. Sadhbh is witty and makes her Mam laugh regularly.

SHADES OF GREY

Saoirse Ní hAgáin

With childhood there is innocence, but sadly the innocent childhood memories I once held so dear are now gone forever . . .

The wind blows the leaves across my feet as I inhale the December air. I can smell Christmas already. I stroll back up the empty road and darkness surrounds me. I think of the holidays and all that comes with it. I turn the corner with a big smile plastered across my face. But it quickly disappears as my mind wanders back over the past year.

Who am I? you might ask. Well, I go by the name Aliah Divine. You see, when I was two years old, my birth parents, Daniel and Grace Divine, died suddenly. Now, at the age of eighteen, when other teenagers my age are going to college, I have made it my goal to find out who my birth parents were and who I really am.

*

As I gently pull the attic door, it creaks with stiffness. What was I thinking? There is no way I can do this! With all my strength, I give a final push and it pops open and flies backwards, leaving a hole big enough to pull myself through.

The rusty ladder creaks under my weight and I stumble

forward. I grab onto the ledge in front of me to steady myself. I put a hand either side and pull myself up.

My foster parents, Elliott and Laura Newbury, would never approve of my snooping. They are firm believers in keeping the past in the past. I knew I forgot something. The flashlight. God, I'm such an idiot sometimes . . .

I remember when I was eight years old and I had just become a member of the Newbury family. At the time, my main goal in life was to go exploring. But unfortunately the social worker and I didn't arrive at the Newbury house till 9 p.m. Laura informed me that it was bedtime and, with overwhelming disappointment, I shuffled off to bed without a word. But at 4 a.m., I grabbed my Barbie flashlight and climbed out the window. I walked aimlessly around the gardens until my flashlight died. I sat quietly in the dark for hours. That night, a feeling of emptiness came over me and it still haunts me to this day.

'Aliah.'

A shout travels up the stairs.

'ALIAH!'

Falling down from the attic, I stumble forward towards the stairs. I run down the steps, two at a time.

'ALIAH.'

'Keep your hair on,' I mutter. 'I'm coming.'

I jog down the stairs to see my foster brother, Robert, glaring at me with such intensity that I think I might burst.

At the age of fifteen, Robert Newbury is the youngest member of the household. You would know we weren't brother and sister from looking at us. Robbie is a tall, muscular, handsome young man with a full head of sandy blonde hair. I, on the other hand, have long, wavy, thick black hair that reaches the small of my back. My skin is more tanned and my face is skinner. At five feet, five inches, I just about reach Robbie's shoulder. But the one thing my foster brother and I have in common is our emerald green eyes, and ironically I think my eyes are my best asset!

'Where did you GO?' Robbie says. 'My DAD is coming

home to THIS!' He paces back and forth. 'THIS! Have you seen the PLACE? There's meant to BE A PARTY HERE TONIGHT!'

'Nice to see you too,' I mumble.

Robbie barrels past me and into the kitchen. I can hear the commotion of pots and pans and I know the kitchen isn't going to survive.

I tiptoe in to see him storming around, swearing and cursing. I realise my back is to the wall. I struggle to push forward without being noticed. Rule one when it comes to Robbie is never put your back to the wall or he'll rant at you for the next few hours. Just when I think I'm in the clear, he turns on me.

'AND YOU,' he roars.

As the words leave his mouth, I hear the click of the front door opening and closing. 'Oh thank GOD,' I sigh.

Laura walks in. I slip past her in the doorway, tears blurring my vision. I run up the stairs to the comfort of my room. I can only hope Robbie forgets his anger towards me.

*

The music steadily makes its way toward me as the hundred-and-something-year-old harpist strums the strings very slowly. I feel awkward standing in the ballroom, in my little black dress that I picked up in Pennys for twelve euro, and my black converse. Laura tried to get me to wear a Christian Dior dress but I wasn't having any of it. Laura's *friends* are surrounding me. They're all mingling. A few even try to approach me. I look into the distance behind them and whisper, 'I see dead people. They're all so beautiful. Can't you see them?'

It gets rid of them quick enough and it is quite amusing at the same time! I look around the jam-packed room, dying to see a familiar face. Of course, I see Tye. Tyler Newbury is the middle child of the family. Like his brother, Robert, Tyler was born with sandy blonde hair, but him being an 'emo' (without the cutting), he dyed his hair black. His fringe hangs low over his right eye and the rest of his hair is covered by his black hood even though we are indoors. His grey skinny jeans cling tightly to his waist and his Vans finish off his outfit. He has his earphones in and while he stands there, his amazingly deep blue eyes flicker back and forth as if paranoid.

I can't just walk up to Tye and say, 'HEY! What's up?'

He would give me one of his *don't talk to me* looks and then he would sigh dramatically and mope to the other side of the room.

I take another desperate sweep of the room and note how beautifully snobby the people surrounding me are. The women stand there, so desirable to all males in the vicinity, and I suddenly feel my self-confidence slipping away. I keep my eyes diverted to the ground and curse myself for not wearing Laura's dress.

I shuffle off to the other side of the room. At a certain point during my walk of shame, a tap lands heavily on my shoulder. I twist around quickly to see Phil standing there with a boyish grin on his face. Philip Newbury is the oldest member of the family. At the age of twenty-two, he doesn't live at home anymore. Last year, just before my eighteenth birthday, he had a massive bust-up with Laura and Elliot. He never said what it was about, but anytime I asked him why he was moving, he would just say he was sorry and that he couldn't handle it anymore.

As he stands here, I can see that he hasn't really changed. His overgrown brown hair still irritates his blue-green eyes and his smile is still as amazing as it was the day he left. Phil was always my favourite. For some reason he always looked out for me.

'Well well, isn't it Miss Aliah,' he smiles, pulling me in for a hug.

'Phil,' I whisper in shock. 'Where have you been? I've missed you so much!'

'I know, Princess, I'm sorry. It's just that—'

'Aliah,' Laura says, interrupting our conversation. 'You can go now. You've put in your appearance.'

I look back and forth between Phil and Laura, unsure what I should do.

'Go,' Phil mouths to me and smiles.

I turn and walk away. On my way out, I grab my car keys off the hall table and slam the door behind me.

*

I pull up in front of a cafe so nicely named *Eurotrash*. I grab my bag and casually stroll through the front doors. I slide into the chair in the corner beside the window and, before I can say *euro*, the waitress, so originally named Betty, is all over me.

'What can I get you, hun,' she says, getting her pencil at the ready.

'Em, just water please,' I reply.

'Water, hunnie? I don't make my living from people ordering water.'

'Em, then can I have a Coke?' I ask.

'Coke,' she sighs, 'yeah, one Coke coming up.'

'Oh, em, sorry,' I call after her, 'is there internet here?'

'Internet?' She stops. 'Yeah, but it will cost ya, hun.'

'Of course it will,' I mutter. I pick up my bag and make my way towards the computers. I let Betty know that I'm moving and choose the computer furthest away from the tables of people. I put the money in the machine and type in Google. The search engine pops up and I type in my father's name, Daniel Divine. I scroll down the page and search through Flickr accounts, Facebook accounts, You Tube accounts and even Twitter accounts. They are all too recent, too new. I need to go deeper.

'Here you go. One Coke,' Betty interrupts. 'Just don't spill it on the computer.'

'Oh, okay, thanks.' I smile

Betty turns to serve the girl next to me. I Google search *National Library Archive* and click on the first link that comes up. On the home page, *Family History Research* pops up. I carefully type in *Daniel Divine* and everything checks out. It says he was an only child, that his mother, Mary Divine (nee Kilbride), died when he was fourteen and, at the age of twenty, his father, also named Daniel Divine, died suddenly. It says that at the age of twenty-two he got married to my mother, Grace Divine (nee Kelly).

Kelly? No, that can't be right. It must be a mistake or a coincidence, unless . . .

I remember when I was around twelve years old and Laura's mother, Julie Kelly, came over for a visit. Of course, Phil, Tye and Robbie were all put on display, all perfectly groomed, but I was sent to my room as it was a family occasion. But I remember a gut instinct told me to stay. I left the room but sat on the stairs right outside. The conversation was mostly about the boys and how they were getting on in school, and sports, but when the boys were distracted, the adults got to the grown-up talk. Laura said something that I couldn't catch and they all laughed, Elliot turned to Laura and laughed, 'That's the Laura Kelly I used to know.' Just then, Phil, Tye and Robbie were sent out of the room and I had to run up the stairs before anyone saw me.

I look up and see it's going for ten at night. I shut down the computer. I zip my jacket up and power walk to my car.

*

It was a hot summer day and Laura's mother had joined us for tea in the garden. Rob skimmed rocks across the gentle river and Elliot had just arrived home but he looked almost surprised to see his mother-in-law sitting there. At the time, I thought nothing of it and continued playing with my toys but I remember Julie Kelly leaning forward and whispering something into Laura's ear. Laura became still. She snapped at us to go inside and we all moved silently. But on my way in, my Barbie fell and I stopped to pick it up. *That's when I heard Laura whisper, 'If you ever tell her, you will never see any of them again.' I started to run, leaving my Barbie behind.*

The sun shines through the dusty window. I pull my flashlight out of my pocket and throw it to one side as a precaution. I carefully put one foot in front of another, testing the rotten wood to make sure it is safe. Dust flies with each step and I pull my top up to cover my mouth and nose. White blankets are over the boxes surrounding me and I pull one back carefully, uncovering four boxes with *Philip* written across them. Having a little peep, I see pictures, toys, certificates, awards etc. All belonging to Phil. Moving on with my search, I find old pictures, toys and boxes belonging to Tye and Robbie, but nothing with my name on it. I plop on a wooden crate. Ten years I've lived in this house and I don't even get a poxy box!

I call it a day. With one foot daggling down the hole, I search for the ladder, but in the corner of my eye, a box flashes into view. Pulling myself back up, I crawl frantically towards it, afraid that if I stand up I'll lose sight of it.

When I reach the box, I see *Grace* scrawled on the side of it. My heart hammering in my chest, I pull the lid off and it falls to the ground with a thump. There in the box lies a photo of two girls smiling at one another. I gently pick it up and stare into the familiar eyes that look so much like mine. I turn the photo to see *Grace age 7, Laura age 10, in the park*, written across the back. Not wanting to believe it, I rummage deeper into the box, only to find my baptismal certificate and there, on the piece of paper, where it says *Witnesses* and *Godparents, Laura Newbury* is written.

I stare into the box, wanting a grip on reality. If only this was a dream. Staring back at me is a white envelope with the words *To Laura* written across it. I pull out the card that is inside and it reads:

To Laura,
I hope you have an amazing birthday. Sorry I can't be there.
Thank you so much for all the baby stuff. You're the BEST sister
in the World!
Love you always,
Grace, Daniel and family

'NO!' I cry, falling backwards.

'Aliah,' Laura warns from her bedroom downstairs.

'ALIAH? Is everything okay?' Elliot calls up from his study below.

Their voices surround me but I don't grasp what is being said. The sound of their voices is overpowered by the sound of my heart as my blood rises and my vision is blurred by my tears. But the most dominating sound of all is the voice inside my head screaming at me to get out. GET OUT!

I turn around blindly, knocking everything in my path, falling and clawing my way towards the only light I can see. My breathing turns shallow and my lungs struggle painfully. How could this happen? Two days ago, I didn't have any family; I was alone and I was content with the loneliness. Now, because of my own stupidity, I've uncovered a truth that I don't think I can face. The people that I've lived with for the past ten years are my family. My aunt. My uncle. My cousins. They are my blood. How could they do this to me? My life was never going to a picnic in the park, but they could have made it easier for me, instead they sat back and watched me struggle. Any hope in my life is gone. The light has turned to darkness. To be honest, there was never any light, more like shades of grey, but even that is gone.

I stumble down the ladder.

'Aliah,' Laura cries, trying to help me up.

'DONT TOUCH ME,' I scream. 'DONT EVER TOUCH ME AGAIN.'

'Do NOT talk to me like that,' Laura warns.

'What are you going to do Laura?' I say, jumping to my feet. 'Or should I say *Aunty* Laura,' Laura stands there, paralyzed, the colour draining from her face. 'Aliah,' she whispers, moving forward to grab my hand.

'What's wrong Aunty Laura?' I look up and see Phil standing behind her, his head lowered to the ground. Confusion hits me again. Why is Phil not angry? Why is he not taking my side? But unless . . . Phil is four years older than me. He would have known my parents. This means *he knew all this time!*

'YOU, you knew all along.'

'Aliah,' Phil whispers, his eyes pleading with mine.

'NO. Why would you all do this to me? What have I done to deserve this? All these years.' I turn back to Laura. 'SIX YEARS. Six years you left me in that home! Were you all hoping someone else would take me?' Tears are streaming down my face and I curse myself for that sign of weakness. 'Was I just an INCOVINENCE?'

'Aliah.' Phil grabs my arm.

'Don't talk to me. You knew all this time. You used to sit there and watch me cry every year on the anniversary of my parents' death. You told me that everything would be okay. Does it look okay, Phil? DOES IT?'

'It's not that simple, Aliah.'

'SIMPLE,' I say. 'Simple. Yeah, I bet it's not.'

'You don't understand,' Phil pleads.

'Well, enlighten me then.'

'What?' he stutters. 'Aliah, please don't do this.'

'Do what?' I laugh. 'Find out the truth? But please do tell me one thing, do Tye and Robbie know? Do they know that I'm their cousin, that the Inconvenience is their cousin? Do they? Are they aware of this minor fact?'

'No.'

'Of course not. Of course not. But just one more tiny question. WHY? Why did you keep me a secret? Did I bring shame on the family? Was I the black sheep, the one who is never spoken of? AM I THAT PERSON?'

'No, you were never that person, you are not that person,' Laura says. 'And you were never a secret.'

'Then why? Why did you not tell me we were family?'

'You look so much like her,' Laura whispers. 'When you first came here, your social worker told us not to tell you just yet, to let you settle in first. She told us that the best way to break the news was to break it to the whole family. But as time went on . . .'

'You chickened out.'

'We didn't want to lose you. You're the only part of Grace I have left. Please understand.'

'Well, Laura, what have you got from not telling me?' I say calmly. 'You just lost me.'

I walk forward, head held high. I walk past my cousins, Tye and Robbie, who were listening from the other room. When I reach the front door, I stop. This is the house I grew up in. The last ten years, I lived in this house with these people. But they lied to me and I know if I stay here I will just be lying to myself.

I open the door and step outside. I take in a steadying breath. I have to be by myself, to figure out who I am. I look back at the house. I don't know what is going to happen with the Newburys but for now a bit of space will be good. I walk up the path.

With childhood there is innocence, but sadly the innocent childhood memories I once held so dear are now gone forever.

 Saoirse Ní hAgáin is fifteen and lives in Whitehall with her family. She has two sisters and one brother and is the baby of the family. She enjoys listening to music, reading and tweeting. Follow her on Twitter @freedomyea.

Room 21

Seona Ní Nualláin

It hit me. She, my daughter, opened those tiny eyes of hers and stared at me. It was incredible, unbelievable, almost like someone had stolen my own mother's eyes and given them to her as a 'welcome to the world' gift. I hadn't thought about my mother for a while; in my opinion, she was gone, finished. I didn't need her, but those eyes triggered something within me; I missed her.

I left her on the 17th of December, exactly three months after the death of my father. She had taken the 'back to normal' approach too quickly for my liking; she was smiling, talking, and acting as if nothing had changed. She was unbearable to be around, I couldn't handle it. So I packed my bags and left, starting a new life, all alone.

Years later, I found myself in a car, with that same daughter, heading in the direction I'd been avoiding – home. Eventually, I found it. It even had my old swing and seesaw, which looked as if they were now being preserved for the next generation. I took my time as I slowly walked up the stone pathway my father had laid. I knocked on the door, and nervously awaited the woman I had abandoned all those years ago. To my surprise, a young woman answered.

I stood there in silence, not knowing what to say.

'Can I help you?' she asked, after a long, awkward pause.

'I'm looking for my mother,' I said, tentatively.

The young woman's face registered shock but softened almost immediately. The look of utter despair etched on my face spoke for me. She kindly invited me in, sat me down and slowly started to explain the situation. She spoke with great urgency. She said that she had moved into the house years ago. Apparently my mother had developed Alzheimer's, and had started to slowly go mad. The last thing she heard was that my mother was 'recovering' in Elba's hospital and that she was doing well. She gave me a bag and explained that she found it after she had moved in, and decided it would be of worth to someone like me, a family member. In the bag was a diary, an old-fashioned looking notebook filled with my mother's thoughts. I bade farewell to the stranger who had helped me, sat in the car and started reading.

September 24th 1987,

He's gone, it's been a week. We're moving on, I know she hasn't come to terms with it yet, it's understandable, he was her Dad, but he was my husband, my one true love. He was supposed to look after me, 'till death do us part', that's what he said. Well, death has parted us and its time to start afresh.

I followed the lady's precise directions to Elba's hospital. I didn't know what to expect. I arrived at a tired-looking building, parked, and found a very lethargic 'electric door'.

The receptionist was dressed in white – she spoke softly, with authority. I told her who I was and who I was there to see.

She tried to explain the seriousness of my mother's illness, 'Years ago your mother was admitted here after a doctor had suggested that she come here temporarily, for respite, but she hasn't left since.'

She continued talking. I couldn't listen any longer. It was too much to take in.

I ran.

'Miss, Miss, stop,' she pleaded. 'She won't know who you are, she doesn't know anyone.'

I raced down the corridor, I could feel my breath quickening, and I was panicking. Regret, loss, confusion. Everything swirled. Around me I could almost sense the seriousness of what I was about to be faced with. Walls, flowers, numbers, doors, escape! What was actually wrong with her? I came to a sudden halt at Room 21; I saw her. I looked through the tiny window and stared. An old woman, rocking back and forth in apparent frustration, she was senseless, distant, disturbed. This woman, my mother, had lost her connection with everyone and everything around her. Someone needed to help her. I stared through the window and saw everything I'd been missing, and more. My childhood, my happiness, my mother. It was all a blur. It had happened too quickly. My mouth went dry, I couldn't speak. After all the years of wondering, waiting, hoping, this was it. The sight of my mother, the mother I used to know so well, looking so ill, acting so strange, sickened me. How could I have left something so important, so vital, so late? We had had our disagreements but they should have been sorted years before. I had left it too late. I knocked on the window.

She turned back, stared, and saw nothing.

 Seona Ní Nualláin is sixteen. She lives in Ashbourne with her parents, her sister, and her brother. She plays the violin, the piano and the banjo. There's nothing she loves more than a good chat over a cup of tea.

COME SIT WITH ME

Sinead Ní Normain

It was 1996. The year Veronica Guerin was shot dead in her car. The year when 2 Became 1 for the Spice Girls and The Fugees were Killing us Softly. The year when Michael Paige became an unemployed plumber in Dublin due to a dodgy ladder his mate had given him to gutter a gaff out in Howth.

The ladder wouldn't stand properly and the snobby swine who owned the house wouldn't stand in the wind and hold the thing for two feckin' minutes. Mick had no choice, either, he'd do the job or the family wouldn't eat for a week – simple as that.

He risked it and fell off the ladder, breaking his two legs and doing his back in. He was two weeks in the Mater. The best two weeks of his life – his own room, no sharing of the TV, *Match of the Day* all day, every day. Breakfast, lunch and dinner brought to his bedside . . . it was the life. That was until they told him he'd never work as a plumber again. It was a Friday night when a nurse gave Mick the bad news. It broke his heart; plumbing was his life. Mick called his eldest son Conor and asked him to come to see him. He told Conor first as he knew he'd understand. Conor wasn't like Mick at all, he was studying Medicine in Trinity. Conor Paige was the best thing to come outta' Ballymun.

—Da, it'll be grand. You know ma, she'll get a job or sumthin', it'll be grand.

—Ma, get a job? That won't happen, she hasn't lifted a finger all her life, what makes you think she will now?

Conor left his da at five that Saturday morning and got a taxi to Balbuther Lane. He hadn't been home in months; he was living it up in Temple Bar with a bird he met in Trinity. Carla, nice girl from Donnybrook studying law like her da.

Conor knocked on the door and his sister Rachel opened it.

—What the hell are you doing here at this hour? she groaned.

—I've been to see da, he's in the Mater, he got bad news tonight.

—Right, OK, come in so, I'll put the kettle on.

Conor sat on the couch waiting for his sister. A few minutes later she arrived in carrying a tin tray with two cups and a few custard creams. She sat beside him and they waited in silence until everyone else came down.

—Ma? Rachel said.

—Rachel, what's wrong, tell me?

—Dad's allowed home. He rang Conor who's just been in to see him.

—But that's good news? Belinda said

—Well there's bad news too ma. The nurse told da he won't be able to work as a plumber ever again, said Conor.

The room went silent. Belinda stood up, got her car keys and drove straight to the hospital. She walked into the ward, where Mick was awake waiting for her. She hugged him through her tears as she sat on the bed. They talked for hours and sort of forgot about what had happened and why they were both there.

—I'll get another job don't you worry, Mick said to Belinda.

He got out of the Mater that evening and Belinda drove home. They stopped in and got chipper in Mr Perri in Santry village and ate it while watching *The Late Late*. The new

Ireland manager, Mick McCarthy, was talking about how he was going to bring Ireland to the top of their game.

—He's a right tosser. I'm off to bed, night love, Mick said.

He hopped up the stairs like a cripple, and got into his own bed. It was just lovely. He slept in the next morning till twelve and when he woke up he felt as if he was still in hospital. Even though he had the telly to himself in the Mater, it was good to be home.

The next morning, Belinda brought him up *The Herald* and a cup of coffee. He was in bed for weeks, flicking through the sports pages, drinking coffee, feeling sorry for himself. Belinda had to get a job and he couldn't even give his youngest daughter Olivia a tenner to go to the cinema. He knew Belinda was getting fed-up running up and down the stairs for him too.

One Sunday morning Mick was flicking through *The Irish Times*. He never read the *Times* as he thought it was a rip-off, but Conor was home and had gone to the shop for the paper. Mick was flicking through the pages, looking at all the boring muck about politicians, bankers and property.

As he was reading about a man who had died in a fire in Galway, something caught his eye in the bottom corner of the page . . . OFFICE ASSISTANT WANTED – NO EXPERIENCE REQUIRED, CALL (01) 8428131.

It would be the answer to all Mick's prayers: a job that involved little movement. He grabbed the phone from the bedside table and called the number. A man answered

—Hello, McCabe Accountants, James speaking. How may I help you?

His voice was clear and perky, as if he'd been answering phones all his life.

—How'ya, I'm lookin' to apply for the job as an office assistant. Do I have the right place?

—You do indeed sir; I'll put you straight on to our HR department.

—Eh, grand, thanks.

Mick was put on hold and this lovely music started playing, like the music on Aer Lingus planes.

—Hello, Julia speaking, how may I help you?

—Hiya Julia, my name is Mick I just read your ad in the *Times* and I'd like to apply for the job.

—Brilliant. Tell me a bit about yourself.

—Well I'm forty and I fell off a ladder about two months ago. I was a plumber. I can't go back to it now so I'm unemployed and looking for a job.

They spoke for about forty minutes and Mick really liked your one Julia. She told him all about the job and the company and how her husband James had inherited it when his da died. She was from town, the Southside. Mick couldn't believe it but she was dead on. Before he knew it he had a job with what seemed like a sound couple on Grant's Row just beside Merrion Square. He was over the moon. Belinda was over the moon, everyone was over the feckin' moon.

Belinda made pasta bake that night and everything felt just right. Mick was starting that Monday, so on Sunday morning he drove down to Ballymun Shopping Centre and got himself a bus ticket for the week. He got his wedding suit steamed in the dry cleaners.

—Belinda love I'm off to work, he chirped up the stairs on Monday morning. It felt good that he could finally say that, knowing he was bringing the bread home. It made him feel like the man of the house again. Off he went to the number 4 bus stop. The 4 left him on Mount Street and he was able to walk straight around to the office, finding it no problem. It was one of the lovely Georgian houses and it had a gold-plated sign on the front door, McCABE ACCOUNTANTS. Mick buzzed the bell and a woman of about forty came to the door. She had lovely chocolate-brown hair with blonde streaks going through it and a little red number on her. Very classy altogether.

—Hi, I'm Mick, your new assistant.

—Oh, welcome Mick. I'm Julia, we spoke on the phone. Follow me to where you'll be doing most of your work, you can leave your coat there.

She pointed at a gold coat hanger

—Lovely, thanks a mil.

Julia showed him up to a little room with a desk and one of those chairs that spin around and hundreds upon hundreds of letters. She handed him a contract and Mick sat down and read it as she looked over his shoulder.

—£16.30 an hour, Jesus Christ I've hit the jackpot! Not bad for someone who's going to be licking envelopes all day.

Mick signed the contract and Julia walked out the door with it in her hand and turned to him while flicking her hair.

—Start filing those letters, please.

She walked away quietly and sat in the office next to Mick's. Mick was there for what seemed like years doing the same thing over and over again. They could have had a feckin' robot to do the job, it was that easy. Mick finished work at six that evening and stood in the pissing rain until the number 4 came around the corner about twenty minutes later. There was no traffic, so Mick wasn't too angry about having to get a bus at forty-five years of age. He got home an hour later and walked in the door to the smell of Belinda's chicken pie.

—Ah, love, you must be psychic. I've been craving chicken pie all day, Mick shouted in to the kitchen from the couch.

—No, love, I'm not psychic, she replied, you texted me earlier.

Mick chuckled and continued to eat his pie. He fell asleep in his suit on the couch and woke up at three in the morning to some tele-shopping crap. He switched off the box and sauntered up to bed.

*

Weeks went past and Mick felt as if he was living the same day over and over again. Monday came around before he knew it and, as usual, Mick got the bus to work. One Monday, as he was walking up Grant's Row finishing his smoke, he heard a scream. A scream a baby would make. Mick noticed it was coming from the office. He walked up the marble steps to the office door, and saw Julia grab her bag. She was the one who was crying. She flew past him with her coat in her hand, wiping mascara from under her eyes. Mick was at a loss. What was he supposed to do? He knew nobody else in the office. He'd never spoken to anyone but Julia. He walked in and the place was deserted. Mick went upstairs and sat in his office. Julia had left him a note saying 'please file all of this before tonight, thanks Julia'. There was a massive pile of files. Mick sat down and put his head in his hands. He sat there for a good ten minutes feeling sorry for himself before finally starting to work. Once he got his filing mojo, he was flying. He had his Discman on and he was listening to his Bagatelle CD. The girls had got it for him for Christmas one year. Hours and hours flew past and Mick's pile got smaller and his arms got tired but he wanted to finish it all before nine. It was about twenty past ten when Mick went down to get his coat.

As he left he heard someone crying in the office. He stopped moving for a minute, trying to work out who it was. It was a fella. Mick didn't know any men in the office but he thought that maybe he should go in to check your man was alright. He opened the door quietly and looked around. The office was full of smoke. The ceilings and walls were yellow from it, there was a Sinatra record playing and a small drinks cabinet beside the record player. Mick couldn't see anyone, he could only hear him. He looked around and then saw something under the table, it was the fella. He got down and sat beside him.

—Y'alright pal? Mick said.

Your man looked at him, got up and poured Mick a drink.

Mick took the drink from him and drank it. Your man poured him another drink and Mick drank that too. They both sat under the table for the rest of the evening listing to Sinatra, singing along and drowning each other's sorrows. Not a word was said, but it was clear the men were unhappy and needed to vent this. At a quarter past twelve Mick stood up and shook the man's hand. The man looked at him for a second and, holding on to Mick's hand, pulled himself up with it to hug Mick. As they both stood there hugging each other, the man whispered into Mick's ear.

—Thanks, I needed that.

Mick walked away. He called a taxi over and got into it. He sat in the back seat half-asleep, wondering what the feck he'd tell Belinda. The taxi pulled up outside the house and Mick handed the taxi driver £35. He hopped out and took baby steps all the way from the garden gate to the hall door. He turned the key really carefully because he knew if he woke Belinda up she'd go ninety the minute he got in the door.

—YESSSS, he silently thought.

That was until he turned around to see her standing at the kitchen door in her nightgown, a look of death in her eye.

—Belinda, love. What are you doing up? Mick asked.

—Mick, love, she said sarcastically, I was about to ask you the same question

—Late night, you know yourself.

Mick knew it was a bad move to say that. He knew she'd go on a mad one now.

—Who the hell do you think you are lying to me Michael? The smell of drink off you. You've clearly been out drinking while I'm sitting at home worrying about the mortgage and feeding the children.

—Love, I'm sorry. It's not what it looks like.

—Yeah, I know love. I'm off to bed and don't bother following me.

Mick slept on the couch that night and got up the next morning in the same clothes. He walked out of the house.

He didn't even brush his teeth. He couldn't, sure. If he walked up the stairs and woke Belinda she'd throw a freaker. So he just left, it was easier on everyone.

Mick got to work on time, and let himself into the office. Julia wasn't there again today. As he filed all day long he tried to put the pieces together as to why Julia wasn't in work. Why was she crying and why was your man in the office drowning his sorrows with a bottle of whiskey? Mick thought they might have been married and it was all going wrong. Mick was right. That afternoon he was finished all his filing so he knocked on the door of the office he was in last night to tell the fella he was leaving, as he seemed to be the only person left in the building.

—Sorry sir, I'm . . .

The man interrupted Mick and told him to sit down beside him; this was the first time Mick had really heard him talk.

—I'm James, by the way; I own this place. Well my da left it to me ten years ago when he died.

—Hiya James, I'm Mick and I've been working for you for the past six weeks.

—Jesus, I'm sorry I never introduced myself to you at the start, I'm a bit of a mess.

With that, James started crying.

Mick rolled a smoke for both of them and they sat under the table once again in silence. They drowned each other's sorrows. It became a bit of a habit. They frequently changed the album. One day it was The Beatles, the next day it was Neil Young. They smoked and drank until they were both so drunk the feeling of pain was numbed. Mick loved every minute of it. It was his new guilty pleasure. He enjoyed staying and sitting with someone who was in the same boat as he was; except James was a hundred grand richer! But that didn't really matter, they didn't judge each other at all, they sometimes didn't even talk, they just sat there.

It was the weekends Mick dreaded now, as he had to stay at home with Belinda. If he even attempted to go out without her she'd start a row about how they never saw each other because he was doing so much 'overtime', as Mick liked to call it. He kinda felt bad for Belinda but then again he didn't.

It was Monday again and Mick was over the moon. He left the house five minutes early. He couldn't wait to go to the office, get his work done, clock out and sit with James for the night listing to some classics. Mick buzzed in at five to nine he was early. James didn't answer, Julia did, and she didn't look too happy.

—Morning Michael, she said sharply. Straight up to your office please and don't leave until you're finished. Is that clear?

—Very.

For the first time in Mick's life a woman had scared him. He walked straight up the stairs, didn't even stop to take his coat off. He felt as if he was walking on broken glass. He didn't listen to his Discman, he didn't go and make himself a cup of tea. He got straight into it, and had finished everything at about half four. He popped into Julia's office but she was gone. He called her name a few times and when she didn't reply he felt he had the all-clear to go down to James.

—Jamesssss, he whispered in the door. It's Mick, can I come in?

—Yeh, the voice was coming from under the table once again.

Mick tiptoed into the office like a child. He got an awful shock when he saw the state James was in. He was unshaven and his hair was wild and sticky out. His shirt had sick stains all over it and his eyes were bloodshot. It looked as if James hadn't been home all weekend.

Mick left the room and went into the kitchen. He got a cloth and some hot water and on his way back from the

kitchen he picked a shirt and comb out of a box of clothes
that had been lying around since Mick had started. Mick put
the box on the table and picked James up and sat him on
the chair. James seemed to be slipping in and out of
consciousness.

　—I'm going to clean you up in case a client sees you like
this.

　—Why do you care about my clients?

　—Because if you stuff up with them they won't use your
service which puts you out of a job and more importantly
me out of a job.

Before James could speak again, Mick took his stained
shirt off him and put the fresh one on. He got the cloth, put
it in the hot water and cleaned James's face up. He then
combed his hair and James looked ten times better. He fixed
them both a cup of tea and for the first time ever they sat on
chairs. James told Mick all his problems and how he couldn't
take Julia anymore. He had only married her in the first
place for her looks. He hated her parents and he also hated
his parents for leaving the company to him. He had had
dreams to travel the world.

　—Are you going to leave her? You must be mad, she's great!

　—Come out with me tonight Mick and we'll have a laugh?
James said to Mick.

Mick was hesitant at first. He didn't know if it was right or
wrong to go but at this stage James was a mate and he felt
he had to.

　—Yeah sure, where to?

James paused and stood looking at the ground with a
smirk on his face. He was still just a little bit drunk.

　—I know a place, get your jacket.

Mick went up to get his jacket and when he came back
down the stairs James was sitting in a taxi outside the
office.

　—Lapello on Dame Street please, James said in a clear
voice.

—Lapello? Mick said in hushed tones so the taxi man wouldn't hear him.

It was a short drive and James handed the taxi man a score and told him to keep the change. James and Mick walked in past the bouncers no problem. They both sat down on a sofa and a waitress came over. James ordered two whiskeys for both of them. Mick felt bad sitting down there looking at women in half nothing. He kept thinking about Belinda, who had texted him earlier to go down to The Towers for a drink after work.

—Damn, I never replied to her about that.

There'd be murder when he got home.

He sat there trying not to look at the women; he kept trying to talk to James. Mick really felt that the two of them should be across the road in The George or something. Mick kept worrying that people thought they were together and that he might see someone he knew. At about half two he got his jacket, finished his drink and dragged James out of the club. James started to sing and of course Mick joined in, the two of them sitting on the steps of the Central Bank singing their hearts out. Eventually James flagged a taxi down and they hopped in. The taxi drove towards James's house and about ten minutes later they were outside a mansion. Mick couldn't believe it; the house had two big pillars and a giant gate.

—Fancy, Mick thought to himself. Very fancy.

James was rooting for his wallet and he took out a fifty pound note and handed it to the taxi driver. Then he went to hug Mick goodbye and instead he kissed him. The two of them sat there for about half a minute. From the corner of his eye Mick saw a light turn on in the house and he pushed James off him. He looked up at the window and saw Julia standing there.

—Damn, she saw that, Mick thought to himself.

James got out of the taxi without saying a word; Mick closed the door after him.

—Just wait a sec pal, make sure he gets in alright, you know yourself.

The taxi man waited and Mick watched James walk up the drive. He watched him ring the doorbell again and again. Mick watched for a good five minutes.

—Balbuther Lane, please, Mick said to the taxi man, still looking at James crying on his doorstep.

Mick arrived home that night and got straight into bed without saying a word to Belinda about the strip club or kissing James or any of the crap that went on. He lay there with her and thought about how he'd miss sitting under the table.

Sinéad Ní Normaín is sixteen and lives with her Mam, Dad and younger brother Niall. Her lucky number is 206. She hates playing camogie, and animals.

A BLOODY HAMMER IN A RUSTY TRANSIT VAN

Stiofán Mac Giolla Rua

'Would yih ever get off!'
Deco was at the end of a four man 'pile on'.
'GERROFF WOULD YIZ!'
Paddy, Skully and Gooky got off.
'It's only a laugh Dec, take a chill pill,' Skully said.
'Yeah yeah I know, just c'mon,' he replied. The four lads strolled across Mellows Park, Finglas. Deco and Skully were sixteen, Paddy was fourteen and Gooky was fifteen.
'Lads, I'm getting a few cans off Vinny on Wednesday,' Paddy proudly exclaimed. Vinny was Paddy's older brother. Vinny, was a tool.
'Paddy you're fourteen for Jaysus sake. Just cop on would ya?' Skully said. Paddy lay silent. He tried constantly to impress the older lads, but sometimes went a bit far. They came to what the lads called 'the van'. It was actually an old abandoned 1989 Transit van without an engine. They hopped in. Deco always sat in the driver's seat and Skully got the passenger's seat with the others left in the back. Paddy's phone rang.
'Hello? Yeah . . . ah here now . . . grand . . . bye-bye-bye.'

'Who was that?' Deco asked.

'Me aul one. Wants me home.'

'Think I'll split too,' said Gooky. Deco and Skully looked at each other.

'We're gonna stall it here.' They all got out of the van, hands were shook and the two lads walked off.

'So what now?' said Skully.

'Dunno, think it's time we really took a look at this piece of metal.' Deco opened the back of the van and Skully searched the inside. 'Nothing. Nothing at all.' Deco rounded the car and went to the boot. It was locked. 'Skully!' he shouted. Skully came around to him.

'Looks like nobody ever searched in here.' Skully's initial instinct was to put his foot through the window, but Deco had a better idea. He disappeared into the van for a minute and came out with an umbrella, battered and ripped, and gave it to Skully. Skully looked up and Deco nodded. Skully smiled.

'AAGGGGGGHHHHHH!'

The echo of Skully's roar could be heard for miles as he rammed the umbrella into the back window, directly over the boot. Deco looked in. Nothing in there other than tubing, a hammer, a tyre and a soaking muddy blanket. 'Ugh, only crap in here.' Skully pulled out the tyre and tubing and Deco took the hammer, leaving the blanket. The first thing you'd think if you had tubing and a tyre is tyre swing, right? But for Skully it was anything but. He took out his lighter and set them alight. This was normal for Skully; he loved fire, always had. Deco walked over and joined him. They sat at the fire until the black smoke of the tyre died down.

'Right,' said Skully. 'Game on.'

'What?' Deco was puzzled by Skully's statement.

Skully ran over to the van, picked up the hammer and threw it. They watched the hammer float through the air. It hit the ground. 'That it? Jeez, go to the gym or something,' Deco said, laughing at Skully's attempt.

'Think you can do better?' said Skully.

'Try me,' said Deco. Skully ran to fetch the hammer. He was back in a flash, he was always a fast runner but he was just a tad bit too lazy to join any athletics. He came back panting, showing how unfit he had become.

''K, go,' he handed the hammer to Deco, who was still sniggering at his feeble throw. Deco paused, then ran a bit and flung the hammer. Deco smiled, happy with his throw, but suddenly his face dropped. He noticed that the hammer was slowly making its way towards a flock of birds. It felt like forever until the hammer finally fell. The birds scattered. Deco ran over and gasped. There lay a crow with its neck half ripped off from the impact of the hammer, which was now covered in the blood of the poor creature. 'Damn. Damn. Damn!' Skully ran over. 'Ahhhhhhh man,' he turned away, unable to look. 'Not cool,' he winced as he looked back at the bird again. 'Not cool.'

'It's not like I meant to do it!' Deco rounded on him, upset at what had happened. Skully went to get the hammer, which was still dripping with the bird's blood.

'C'mon, stall ih,' Skully said, heading back towards the van. Deco followed. As they reached the van Deco sighed, thinking about life and how fast it could end without even seeing it coming.

'Snap out of it eejit!' Skully cried. He threw the hammer to Deco, who wrapped it in the muddy blanket, then chucked it in the back of the van again, before the pair left for home.

*

Two days later. Deco still had the death of the bird on his conscience, not that he cared, just that he had taken the life of another living creature. He glanced at the clock. 9:45 p.m. It was just him, like it usually was. His parents had gone out to the pub and his brother had gone to his girlfriend's house who lived all the way out in Maynooth.

'Ah here Black Ops time,' he said, picking up the Playstation 3 controller.

BANG!

Before he could even start a match, a loud noise shook him and two men dressed in black, holding guns, burst into the room. It was a raid. Deco was lifted, handcuffed and brought through his hall and out the front door, which had been ripped off its hinges. Outside, more men, armed with batons, were staring at him. Neighbours at their porches, curtins twitching, flashes of light, his feet not quite touching the ground as he was half walked, half marched down the driveway. Blue sirens, a white police car, then next thing he knew he was tossed inside, literally thrown, as if he were yesterday's discarded paper. In the space of a minute and a half Deco had been arrested.

11:06 p.m. and Deco was still waiting. He had been in the interrogation room in Pearse Street Garda Station for ages. Finally two Gardai burst through the door and flung someone else into the room with him.

'DECO! THE HELL ARE YOU DOING HERE?' it was Skully. Deco had never been happier to see him.

'Dunno man. They just charged into me gaff and here I am.'

'Same here,' said Deco.

'Pigs pure stormin' the place,' said Skully. 'Lifted me up. Before I knew it . . .' Skully trailed off as three men entered the room.

'Declan Tiernan and Peter O'Neill. I hope we didn't keep you waiting,' said one of them. Skully had no time for Guards.

'Yeah? What's it to ye?' he sneered.

'We've just received your profiles.' The man studied a piece of paper in his hand. 'I believe you go by the names of Deco and Skully. I can understand the nickname Deco but why Skully?'

'Why Skully?' Skully snapped. 'You bring me into this kip for no good reason at all hours of the night, and all you want to know is how I got my nickname? Well I'll tell you why. It's because I love SMASHING THE THICK SKULLS OF YOU

PIGS OFF BRICK WALLS ISN'T IT!' The man let out a sigh.
'We'll see how far that behaviour will get you,' he said.
Deco stood, put his hands on the table in front of him and
took a deep breath.

'Never mind him,' he said. 'He gets mad a lot. Now would
you kindly mind telling us why you brought us here?' The
man stood up.

'With pleasure. My name,' he flashed his badge, 'is
Sergeant Kavanagh, and we brought you here tonight
because the two of you are prime suspects in a murder case
we are investigating.'

'Say what now?' Skully shot to his feet, as did Deco beside
him, but the men pushed them back down in their seats.

'We found a weapon,' said Sgt Kavanagh, 'at the scene.
Covered in both of your fingerprints.' Skully and Deco's
jaws dropped. Sgt Kavanagh turned to one of his colleagues
and asked for the weapon. Deco's head was spinning. What
type of evidence were the Garda were trying to plant on
him? And why? He hadn't killed anyone. He watched as Sgt
Kavanagh laid a plastic transparent bag on the table in front
of them. Inside it was a hammer smeared in blood. A bloody
hammer. A bloody hammer from a rusty transit van.

Deco and Skully looked at each other. Deco smiled.
Himself and Skully sat back in their seats.

'You obviously haven't looked into this have you?' said
Deco. The Sergeant looked confused.

'We have your fingerprints all over this hammer and it's
covered in your blood! We have you! We know your type!'
he shouted. 'You're not getting out of this.'

'No!' Deco shouted. 'You clearly don't know our type!
You're so sure about us and stereotyping us that you haven't
even considered what blood that is!' The Sergeant's eyes
widened. He turned and whispered to one of the men. The
man got up, took the hammer in the transparent bag and
left. Approximately a minute later the Sergeant and the
other man left too.

'Holy crap,' said Deco.

'Me heart nearly stopped there,' said Skully.

'Yeah I know what you mean,' said Deco, 'but still, play it straight, anything could happen.'

*

1:00 a.m. The Sergeant entered the room at that exact time, alone, with an agitated look about him.

'So we checked the blood sample and it appears you were right. The blood trace on the hammer wasn't human; it was from a jackdaw. You win.' It killed him to admit it, but no more could be done. 'You're free to go,' the Sergeant indicated the door.

'Hang on a minute,' Deco shouted. 'You've accused us of murder, stereotyped us and brought us in here for absolutely no reason and that's all okay? I feel a complaint is in order.' Sgt Kavanagh sighed.

'How much?' he said.

'A grand,' said Skully. 'Each. And a new front door for Deco.' The Sergeant groaned.

'Done,' he said.

*

Deco and Skully walked down the hall of Pearse Street Garda Station, smiling and grinning at every Garda that walked by until they came to the end of it where Deco reached out, opened the door, and took the long awaited deep breath, of freedom.

Stiofán Mac Giolla Rua was born and raised in Dublin. He's sixteen and lives with his Mam, his Dad and his sister, Sorcha. He enjoys playing piano and the uilleann pipes. People tend to call him Stee and he likes going to Shay's house on Wednesdays, with Alex.

THANK YOUS

Trish de Bhál, Sarah Tully, Helen Seymour, Adrienne Quinn, Paul Singleton, Anne Parsons, Caroline Heffernan, Sara Bennett, Orla Lehane, Caroline McMahon, Alan Bennett, Sophie Martin, Daragh O'Toole, Joanne Hayden, Jean Hanney, Vinnie Quinn, Ciara Doorley, Daniel Bolger, Declan Meade, Anne Enright, Roddy Doyle, Cormac Kinsella, Ray Lynn, Emmy Lugoye, Lisa Essuman.